THE WATCHING WOOD

Praise for
THE demon notebook

'a spookily bewitching story' *The Irish Times*

'the teen dialogue is sharp and realistic, an excellent read'
Irish Examiner

'thrilling story full of twists for older readers' *Primary Times*

Praise for
THE broken spell

'the multi-layered plot bounds along breathlessly, with crisp
schoolgirl dialogue… the eccentric new characters make for an
Irish Hogwarts' *Irish Examiner*

'a very exciting read that offers young readers something to
think about as well as something to make them jump'
Books for Keeps

'with sharp observations and perceptive descriptions ... the teen
dialogue is spot on' *Irish Independent*

Erika McGann grew up in Drogheda and now lives in Dublin. As a kid she wanted to be a witch, but was no good at it, so now she spends her time writing supernatural stories, and living vicariously through her characters. She hopes, in time, to develop the skills to become an all-powerful being. *The Watching Wood* is her third book.

THE WATCHING WOOD

... beware the eyes in the dark ...

ERIKA McGANN

**Winner of the Waverton Good Read
Children's Award 2014**

THE O'BRIEN PRESS
DUBLIN

First published 2014 by The O'Brien Press Ltd,
12 Terenure Road East, Rathgar, Dublin 6, Ireland.
Tel: +353 1 4923333; Fax: +353 1 4922777
E-mail: books@obrien.ie
Website: www.obrien.ie

5845665.

ISBN: 978-1-84717-682-0

8 7 6 5 4 3 2 1
18 17 16 15 14

Layout and design: The O'Brien Press Ltd.
Cover and internal illustrations by Emma Byrne
Printed and bound by CPI Group (UK) Ltd, Croydon, CR0 4YY
The paper in this book is produced using pulp from
managed forests.

he O'Brien Press receives financial assistance from

CONTENTS

dedication

For my mum, for being wonderful

acknowledgements

Many thanks to my lovely editor, Marian Broderick, for all her work over the last couple of years – I can't believe it's the third book already! I'd like to thank my sister, Kunak, for helping to get my books across the ocean, Emma Byrne for the fabulously creepy cover, and everyone at O'Brien Press.

1

Flaming Feet

Grace Brennan's feet pedalled furiously in the air below her. She was exhausted. Sweat dampened her shirt, and all she could think about were those women who sat on exercise bikes in the window of her local gym, spinning like their lives depended on it.

'Don't slow down, Grace, you're nearly there!' Ms Lemon's voice sounded from the ground beneath.

The effort of staying airborne in one spot was starting to wrench at Grace's gut and her legs were ready to give in, when a sudden spark singed her ankle and a sweeping blue flame surged from the heel of each foot to the toe.

'Agh! My feet are on fire!'

'Excellent, that's perfect!' Ms Lemon yelled. 'Now, run!'

Grace lurched forward, her tired legs feeling detached

from her body as she raced just ahead of the fire. The hot blue cooled to orangey yellow as she left a trailing flame across the dusky sky, ducking to avoid the curly fire-trails left by Rachel and Jenny's flame-running contest.

'Watch this one,' Jenny called from above, her athletic frame silhouetted by the sun.

Picking up speed, she ran downwards then back up, fast enough to turn a tight loop-the-loop, leaving a fading circle of fire in her wake.

'Aw, come on,' Rachel complained, shaking her layers of shiny dark hair. 'That's it, I'm going back down. I'm wrecked.'

In a gentle slope towards the field below, Rachel slowed her pace until the fire at her feet extinguished in two puffs of smoke, and she landed gracefully in the grass. She was rewarded with applause from Ms Lemon, and a derisive snort from Mrs Quinlan. Grace envied Rachel's elegance. She was like a cat, always landing on her feet. With her own limbs barely under her control, Grace felt like a flying St Bernard. Wiping a sheen of sweat from her freckled cheeks, too late she spotted a speeding object, with a short black bob, that came suddenly thundering towards her.

'Look out in front!' Una shrieked before smashing into Grace hard enough to snuff out both their flames.

They spun towards the ground, arms and legs akimbo, until Grace, with the last bit of strength she had, hissed a verse and produced enough of a flying spell to slow their descent. They still hit the ground pretty hard. Una rolled off Grace, groaning in pain.

'That hurt!'

'You landed on *me*,' Grace replied, rubbing her bruised head.

'Oh, I'm sorry,' Una's hand went back, but didn't quite reach Grace's. 'Are you broken?'

'I'll live.'

Una rolled towards her, wrinkling her little upturned nose with a smile.

'You're a legend.'

'I know.'

'That was pathetic,' Mrs Quinlan's voice growled behind them. 'Get up and give me fifty star jumps.'

'What?' cried Una. 'They're not magic.'

'Well, you're obviously not fit enough to handle basic flame-running, so I think it's about time we added some circuit training to your lessons.'

'Extra P.E.?' Una's grey eyes watered. 'That's worse than *torture*.'

'I can always arrange both.'

'Maybe we'll start the more energetic lessons with a warm-up jog from now on,' Ms Lemon said diplomatically. 'We don't want anyone pulling a muscle.'

'They've got no muscles to pull,' Mrs Quinlan said over her shoulder, her pale eyes frosty as she walked off the field.

Una lifted her arm to flex her bicep and squeezed it, pulling a face like a boxer in the ring.

'Yeah? Any more mention of star jumps and I'll bring out the gun show.'

'What?' Mrs Quinlan turned.

Una ducked behind Grace.

'Nothing.'

Jenny's purple doc boots slammed into the ground, making them all jump.

'Catch that loop, Rach?'

'Couldn't really miss it,' Rachel said flatly. 'You win this one.'

Jenny interlocked her fingers and stretched her arms to crack her knuckles.

'Ah, nothing like some aerial gymnastics to wind down after a long day.'

'Adie and Delilah,' Ms Lemon called upwards, 'time to come down now.'

'Two minutes, Miss!'

'We're losing daylight here, Adie.'

'I know, I know, Miss, but watch this!'

Grace leaned back on her elbows and watched as Adie and Delilah, hand-in-hand, ran a double trail of flame through the air. Adie wasn't tall, and Delilah was shorter still, and yet they managed to run in perfect sync. Grace watched them work, feeling a little glow at how well Delilah had fit into their group.

Increasing their speed, the two girls turned tightly upwards, making a helter skelter shape that ran almost two storeys high then, at the top, Adie gripped both of Delilah's hands as the smaller girl kicked her legs up and snapped her heels together, topping the giant cone with a burst of bright orange flame.

'Woah!' Una clapped wildly.

Grace sprang to her feet and joined in the cheering.

'Awesome,' Rachel yelled.

'That *was* awesome,' Jenny lamented.

'Ha! You'll win the next one.'

Jenny sighed and joined in the applause as the two flying girls slowed to a stop above them, snuffed out their flames, and hovered for a quick bow. Adie blushed, her almond-shaped eyes sparkling, as she let go of Delilah's hand and dropped towards the ground.

But her feet never touched the grass. As she came in to land, something tubular erupted from the soil underneath her. It sucked in her legs and then the rest of her, before disappearing beneath the ground. There was a yelp, a swish of her black curls, and she was gone. Silence.

Grace stared at the space where Adie had been, then at Ms Lemon. The teacher looked aghast.

'I don't ... I don't know what—'

'*Run!*'

Grace spun around to see Mrs Quinlan sprinting towards

them from the gate. She turned back towards her friends — just in time to see Rachel's horrified expression as she too was sucked down a wormy chute.

'Run, run!' Mrs Quinlan shrieked.

'What's happening?' shouted Grace.

'Shut up and *run*!'

They shot off in all directions, squealing with fright. The ground belched another chute that lunged for Jenny's feet. She just avoided it, reaching the edge of the field and scurrying up a tree. But the tube snaked up the bark, weaving between branches and reaching with swollen lips, until Jenny screamed and launched herself into the air. But she wasn't fast enough. Grace saw Jenny's auburn hair vanish into the mouth of the squirmy cylinder.

Her own collar was snatched by Mrs Quinlan and she was thrown violently onto one of the large rocks that lined the edge of the field. Mrs Quinlan pulled a wooden charm from her pocket, rubbed it vigorously on the stone, and shoved it into Grace's hand.

'Stay there.'

'What are those things? What's going *on*?'

'I don't know,' the woman replied. 'But whatever it is, it's not good. Don't move an inch off that rock.'

Mrs Quinlan took off, grasping Delilah's tiny waist as yet another chute sprang out of the grass. She hurled the small girl in Grace's direction and Delilah scrambled over the stone to clutch her hands. They watched Mrs Quinlan charge across the field with unlikely speed, shouting to Ms Lemon and Una, who were zig-zagging through the trees on the other side. Her long, moth-eaten coat flew out behind her and her frizzy grey hair bounced up and down as she pounded forward. For a second, Old Cat Lady – as the girls had long ago nicknamed her – looked to Grace like a super-hero. A beam of light intermittently flew from her hands, striking a wormy shape that was aiming for Una's feet, and Grace recognised the magical boomerang-like weapon that had saved her from the clutches of the wicked Ms Gold earlier that year.

Riveted by the scene, Grace suddenly lost her balance. Something had hit the rock from beneath, hard enough to split the stone. She toppled to the ground but was pushed back up before she knew what had happened.

'Grace!'

Delilah's wide, brown eyes caught hers for a second, before the tiny girl was sucked into the soil.

'Delilah, no! Mrs Quinlaaan!'

Across the field both teachers stood frozen, staring at the ground. Una was nowhere to be seen.

'Where's Una?' Grace cried. 'Where are they all gone? What's *happening*?'

The two women looked towards her and started running. But it was too late. Another blow from beneath, and the rock splintered into pieces. Grace felt a powerful vacuum at her back, and blue sky was the last thing she saw before everything went dark.

✳ ✳ ✳

'Grace, wake up. Wake *up*.'

Grace swatted at the grip on her shoulder.

'Stop. What are we—'

Adie's worried face and dark curls swam into focus. Past her Grace could see an arched ceiling, supported by huge wooden beams, like the roof of a cathedral. Rachel's porcelain features came into view, then Delilah's dark complexion. Grace was now being shaken by several eager hands.

'Stop!'

'Shh!' Jenny grabbed her beneath the arms and hoisted her to her feet. 'Don't make a sound. We don't know what the hell is going on.'

They were in the middle of a large crowd, broken into groups, surrounded by the stone walls of a grand hall. It wasn't a cathedral – Grace couldn't see any religious stuff anywhere – but there were steps at the front that led to a platform. There stood a rotund woman with thinning blonde curls, wrapped in layers of dark-coloured velvet, gesturing wildly and giving an impassioned speech. Behind her stood an incredibly tall woman, her hands clasped in front. Beside them slouched a diminutive man, so hunched over that the lapels of his brown tweed jacket fell forward.

'– and not without good reason.' Grace was beginning to make out the stout woman's speech. 'Death. Death is the curse and the blessing. Death is what separates the fools from the heroes, the large from the squirmy, and the trees from the teeny whiney weeds. Death is … These Trials are what bring you closer to the … to the honour of the glory, and the glory of the honourable, most honourable glory–'

The tall woman quickly stepped forward.

'We would like to thank Madame Three for her wise and encouraging words.' She deftly steered the shorter woman to the back of the platform.

Grace grasped Jenny's arm.

'Where the *hell* are we?'

'Who spoke?' Madame Three spun out of the tall woman's grip and darted towards the top of the steps. 'Who spoke?'

The crowd turned as one to face Grace. They were mostly kids of secondary school age, and Grace had the familiar and uncomfortable sensation of being singled out at assembly.

'You!' Madame Three jabbed a finger in her direction. 'You *spoke*.'

The tall woman stepped forward with a curious look.

'I don't recognise your coat-of-arms.'

She glided down the few steps to the floor and the crowd parted silently as she made her way through, her heavy skirts of grey lace sweeping over the floorboards. She stopped in

15

front of the six girls and scratched the crest on Jenny's jumper.

'Which school are you?'

Jenny seemed too bewildered to speak. The woman raised her voice sharply.

'Which school are you?'

'St John's,' Grace croaked. 'From Dunbridge.'

The woman's face, creased in confusion, suddenly smoothed as she called out,

'New blood!'

She swept back to the stage and raised her arms with an eerie smile.

'For seventeen generations we three, the Supreme Heads of the Lyceum of Wicca,' she gestured to her companions on the platform, 'have hosted the Trials, and for seventeen generations we have tested the skill and fortitude of the very best students of Wicca. You were hand-picked by your tutors as the fiercest, the most talented, the most intuitive witches in your schools, and now a brand new school,' she paused, glancing upwards as if to remember the name, 'St John's of Dunbridge, have sent us their most esteemed students to compete, to fight and perhaps to die, for the glory of winning this year's Witch Trials!'

Grace raised her hand.

'Eh, sorry ... to what?'

'We didn't get sent,' Una whimpered, also raising her hand. 'We got took.'

The woman either didn't hear or deliberately ignored them.

'In the coming days, those of you more familiar with the challenges that lie ahead may test the fortitude and knowledge of the new bloods. And we, the Supremes, will watch with–'

Una snorted loudly, then clapped her hand over her mouth.

'You dare to interrupt again?'

Una shook her head, but her shoulders were shaking and tears of laughter were forming in her eyes. The woman's colour was rising.

'You dare to interrupt the Lady Hecate during the welcoming speeches. You dare to interrupt the Supremes!'

Una pressed both fists into her face, like she was trying to jam them up her nose. Grace gave her a sharp dig in the ribs.

'Una,' she whispered. 'Don't.'

'They're called the *Supremes*.' Una's voice was muffled. 'Like that girl band from the 60s.' She looked at Grace pleadingly. 'You know, *Stop in the Name of Love* and all that. My dad's got all their CDs.'

The enormous candelabras lighting the hall suddenly flickered all at once, and shadow spread from the platform as Lady Hecate raised her arms.

'SILENCE!'

The sound was more than just voice. It boomed from the walls and the floor, reverberating through the hall and making

Grace weak at the knees. There wasn't a sound from the crowd as the echoes and shadows retreated, and the purple hue faded from Lady Hecate's cheeks. She lowered her arms slowly, her gaze fixed on the girls from St John's. Grace could feel the seething stare of every person in the room. Whatever this Trial stuff was, they were off to a bad start.

'Raise your eyes and pay tribute to those who have gone before you.'

As Lady Hecate spoke, light filled the arched ceiling, illuminating a balcony that ran both sides of the hall. Between the wooden beams stood giant busts – the head and shoulders of various figures – carved in stone.

'Lucinda Grey,' Lady Hecate gestured, as one bust was illuminated brighter than the others, 'Captain of Hawk Falls, the very first champions of these Trials. Grey was champion a second year, before being decapitated in the Blade Room in her third.'

Grace gulped.

'Denton Malorous,' the woman continued, 'led his team to victory no less than three times during his illustrious career. Determined to compete one last time, he was devoured whole by a globular serpent in his final year. Atraya Neubelbaum, victorious in more individual trials than any other competitor in history, though she never held the trophy; impaled on the battlements during an airborne skirmish.'

Jenny squeezed Grace's arm.

'There's a pattern emerging here, and I don't like it.'

'Let's just get through this 'welcoming' thing,' Grace whispered, 'and then figure a way out of here.'

'I got a quick look out the window. Wherever this is, it's nowhere near home.'

Grace stretched onto her tiptoes, just able to get a glimpse of the outside world through one of the arrowslit windows. Back in the field with Ms Lemon and Mrs Quinlan it had still been daylight, but it was well into evening now. In the starlight she could see barren landscape, with a forest in the distance, and a river that snaked through both. It could have been somewhere wild like the Burren if it weren't for the green hue that permeated everything, bleeding through the glassless windows and into the stone of the great hall. Panic grew in the pit of Grace's stomach. Jenny was right. They were nowhere near home.

'So remember the great ones who perished in the name of glory, and brought great honour to their schools.'

Lady Hecate levelled her gaze in the girls' direction.

'And, new bloods, get whatever sleep you can. For tomorrow, the Four Hundred and Twenty-Sixth Annual Witch Trials begin.'

2

THE VENETIAN ROOM

Grace walked gingerly behind the hunched man, trying not to step on his heels. After Lady Hecate had dismissed the crowd, the girls had been left in the charge of the remaining member of the Supremes.

'As new bloods you have the privilege of Lord Machlau's guidance for a tour of the castle,' the tall woman had said as the diminutive man from the platform had ambled towards them. 'Tithon Castle was built according to his strict instructions – there is no nook or cranny of this place beyond his knowledge – and, as you can see, his boundless energy and enthusiasm come alive when discussing its fine buttresses and exquisite arches.'

She had stepped back, allowing the stooped creature with short hair slicked across his forehead, to inch forward and pause in front of the girls. They had all stood silent for a few moments, Lord Machlau's gaze fixed on the floor, before the man had shuffled forward, his tweed lapels swinging as they hung from his bent frame.

'We could make a run for the door,' Jenny whispered as the girls followed their guide from the hall into a winding corridor.

'You know where the front door is?' said Rachel.

Jenny shook her head.

'Let's just get the tour, then we can bolt when we know which direction to bolt in.'

'Even if we do make it outside,' said Grace, 'how do we make it home from there?'

'Yeah,' said Jenny, 'with all that weird greenness out there, I'm thinking we're not in Kansas anymore.'

'Besides, I dunno if you've noticed, but we're not getting much info on this tour.'

As if on cue, Lord Machlau stopped suddenly, his left arm shooting upwards, his head still levelled at the floor.

'South Wing.' His voice was nasal and pinched. 'Wavaged by civil war. Webuilt by the Waven Clan.'

He stood frozen, still pointing towards a dark entrance at the top of a steep flight of stone steps. The silence went on so long Grace thought maybe he was waiting for them to comment.

'That's nice. It's kind of—'

21

The arm snapped back to his side, and the shuffling continued.

'What's wavaged?' Una whispered. 'Does that mean all destroyed and stuff?'

'I think he means ravaged,' replied Grace. 'And yeah, destroyed.'

Another stop and the arm shot out to the left.

'North-east Wing. Inset with pwecious wock from the Daimone Wegion.'

Grace let the pause hang this time, and eventually the tour went on.

'This is going to take all night,' said Jenny.

She wasn't far off. Several hours later, the girls were dragging themselves along behind Lord Machlau's stumpy frame. Despite what looked like considerable physical discomfort, the small man never seemed to tire. Eventually, they came to a narrow canal that cut right through the stone floor and ran upwards to another entrance a floor up. Two mini gondolas bobbed on the water, secured to the edge with lengths of rope. The shooting arm pointed to the boats.

'To the Venetian Woom in the North Wing.'

Grace gazed absentmindedly at the open doorway above, waiting for the sound of dragging feet once more. But the pause didn't end this time.

'I think we're supposed to get in,' Delilah said.

'You will be accommodated in the Venetian Woom.' The

arm still pointed at the gondolas.

'Oh fudge, I think you're right,' said Grace, her weary mind suddenly focussing. 'Hey, that water's moving uphill!'

The canal water was indeed travelling in the wrong direction and, as the girls clambered into the two boats, the ropes were unleashed and suddenly they were speeding away from the frozen figure of Lord Machlau, and through the arched doorway above.

Out of the darkness and through several candlelit rooms, they zigged and zagged along the canal. Grace grasped the curved bow of the gondola with Delilah hanging off one arm and Una gripping her waist.

'I think I'm gonna be sick!' Una said.

Before Grace could answer, the gondola tipped over the edge of a waterfall, plummeted into darkness, then jolted horizontal and sailed to a smooth stop. Like the rest of the castle, the room was lit with large candelabras, but that's where the comfort ended.

'This can't be our room,' said Grace.

They heard distant screams, then a whoosh of water as the gondola carrying Jenny, Adie and Rachel glided to a stop behind them. Adie spilled out of the boat, clutching her stomach.

'Oh God,' she said, 'that was worse than the Death-Defier at Funshine Park.'

'The giant roller coaster?' said Jenny. 'You didn't go on it.'

'Because it looked like it would feel like this!'

'This isn't our room, is it?' Rachel stepped off the boat onto the ledge.

There was no furniture in the room. It was large, but made entirely of stone, with several narrow windows too high to look out of, and a few alcoves tucked into the walls. Aside from the canal they sailed in on, there were six or seven others, crossing and interlocking, though all but two exited through covered drains. A sudden clattering drew Grace's attention to a sign on the wall behind them. She read *The Venetian Room* in blocked wooden letters, then beneath it as more letters snapped into existence, *St John's of Dunbridge*.

'Fudge.'

'It *is* our room,' Adie groaned. 'What are we supposed to sleep on?'

'Why would we sleep?' exclaimed Jenny. 'Let's go find the front door and get the hell out of here.'

'You remember where it is?' asked Grace. 'Because that tour went on forever, and I've no idea where we are right now. We took so many turns, up and down stairs, not to mention the log flume ride. How could we possibly find our way out?'

'And not all the rooms were lit,' said Delilah. 'It will be even harder in the dark.'

'And I don't think I could walk another step,' Una said, flopping down into one of the alcoves.

'Right,' said Grace, 'then we've no choice. Let's get some sleep, wait until daylight, then figure out a plan.'

'Sleep where? I don't see any beds.'

'It's gotta be these things.' Jenny had leapt across two canals, and was leaning on a ledge pulling what looked like white sackcloth from the water. Grace followed her and saw six hammocks – or at least *half*-hammocks – each fixed to a metal hook at one end, with two knotted corners bobbing on the water at the other.

'We're meant to climb on those things? Are they even waterproof?'

'They float,' said Jenny, kicking off her shoes. 'I'll give it a try.'

She eased herself into one of the hammocks, squealing as she nearly tipped into the water, then leaned back and smiled.

'They're comfy!'

'Lemme try.'

Taking off her shoes, Grace put one foot on a hammock and nearly toppled over the side.

'Keep to the middle,' said Jenny, relaxing with her hands behind her head. 'Don't let it tip to one side or the other.'

Using another approach, Grace gripped the metal hook at the ledge, then slid her feet down the sackcloth until she was lying on her front.

'Ooh,' she said, squirming onto her back. 'It's nice. With

the water moving it's calm-like.'

'Yeah, might get one of these when I get home.'

Rachel sank into one with her usual grace, and Delilah's tiny frame seemed barely to rock the hammock as she climbed in. Adie finally managed to settle herself with Grace and Jenny's help but, try as she might, Una couldn't find her balance. She clung to the metal hook, the sackcloth tipping perilously from side to side.

'Just slide down into it, and let go of the edge,' said Grace.

Una lay face down on the cloth, her feet digging into the knotted corners and her knuckles white as she kept her grip on the metal hook.

'Just let go,' Grace said. 'You're lying on it now.'

'I'm fine.' Una's voice was muffled in the hammock.

'You can't sleep like that. Let go, you won't fall in.'

'I said I'm fine like this.'

'You look like you're hanging off the edge of a cliff.'

'I said I'm *fine*.'

'Okay, sorry. I'll shut up.'

The light dimmed suddenly as the flames of the candelabras shrank almost to nothing.

'Guess that's lights out,' said Jenny. 'Night night everyone.'

'Hey,' said Grace, 'do you think some of the other kids might help us out tomorrow? Maybe they know how we can get home.'

'Yeah, cos after that assembly thing, I think they love us.'

Grace curled up into the surprising comfort and warmth of the hammock.

'You never know.'

'Go to sleep, Brennan.'

''Night.'

Some time later, Grace awoke with a start as something splashed into the water.

'Oh God, Una, was that you?'

'I hate these stupid things!' Una snarled, doggy paddling to the edge and dragging herself out of the canal. 'And my hands are all sore.'

'Were you holding on this whole time? Oh Una, you can't sleep on the stone, you'll freeze. You're soaking wet.'

'Where else am I supposed to sleep?' the girl snapped.

'Well then, take my jumper at least.'

Everyone peeled off any extra layers and Una, still shivering in a change of clothes, crawled into one of the alcoves and didn't speak for the rest of the night.

✳ ✳ ✳

In the morning, the candelabras flared bright again, the arrowslit windows being too high and too skinny to let in much daylight. Grace held her breath as she stuck her mobile in the air one more time but … nothing. She had hoped the morning would bring one of them signal, but no such luck. She switched hers off to save battery.

Not sure how else to leave the room, the girls climbed back into the gondolas, which immediately took off. They took a different route though, depositing the girls in a hallway filled with oil paintings, portraits and dusty old furniture, where many of the crowd from the day before were also arriving. From there, they were herded into a huge dining room, where people were already seated at long tables, digging into breakfast. There were student prefects at each corner of the room, shoving trays into peoples' hands and yelling at that them to sit down and be quiet.

Grace took a tray and filed into the queue for food. Like most school cafeterias, nothing looked too inviting.

'Algae mash?' a bored canteen lady asked, her ladle filled with something blueish and gooey.

'Um, sure.'

Grace grimaced as the oozy mush was slapped onto her plate. She turned down the slimy strings that looked like celery boiled in mud, and the steak that was a little too yellow for her liking. At a scowl from the canteen lady, she finally accepted two of the round, brown ovals that might have been potatoes baked for several years. They clattered noisily onto her plate.

With trays full of the most unappetizing slush they had ever seen, the girls headed for six free seats opposite a group of girls in red uniforms, and there was a sudden hush.

'They're sitting with Hawk Falls!' Grace heard someone

whisper. 'How stupid are they?'

The girls in red had stopped eating, and were staring at them with obvious disapproval.

'Hi,' said Grace, 'are these seats taken?'

There was no reply as the other team continued to stare, and the girl in the middle with pixie-short blonde hair dropped her fork loudly onto her plate. She had a pale fur wrapped around her shoulders, which Grace, with a cringe, realised was genuine. The head and legs were still attached, and the eyes stared out, black and glassy, as the head lolled gently at the blonde girl's neck.

'It's nice to meet you,' Jenny said, reaching her hand across the table. 'I'm Jenny.'

'Good for you,' the pixie-cut girl replied, sweeping her own hand down the fur at her throat and standing. The animal head rocked disconcertingly on her shoulder as she moved. The rest of the team followed her lead, and pretty soon everyone sitting within several feet of Grace and her friends got up and left the dining hall.

'Wow,' said Jenny, 'we nearly cleared the room.'

'Think we can rule out getting help from any of them.' Grace's tummy grumbled as she pushed the algae mash around her plate.

As the girls picked at their food, there was a loud clatter and someone staggered into the back of Adie, clipping her on the back of her head with a tray.

'Ow!'Adie rubbed the throbbing spot, already turning into a lump.

'Oh, sorry! I'm so sorry, are you okay?' The dark-skinned girl was very young, about nine or ten, and her hair was tightly twisted into bantu knots. Adie nodded and winced, as the girl backed away holding a loaded tray with an apologetic smile.

'Aura!' her captain snarled. 'No talking.'

The girl trotted towards the dark-haired teenage boy that had spoken, and got an angry-faced telling off from the rest of her team.

'Are you sure you're alright?' A tall boy with strawberry blond hair and a smile that was a little too wide for his face looked down at Adie.

'Oh, em, yeah. Thanks.'

'No problem. I mean, good. I'm glad you're okay.'

Adie's cheeks flushed pink.

'Thanks.'

There was an awkward pause the other girls were too intrigued to break, before the boy spoke again.

'You might want to hurry a bit. The Supremes don't like lateness, and after your– Well, after yesterday ...'

'Oh yeah, thanks. Yesterday, yeah, we were a little–' She rose quickly, her tray smashing into his, tossing plates and food everywhere.

'Oh, fudge, sorry!'

'Sorry!'

'No, that was my fault, I'm so sorry. I'm always so—'

'No, that was me. I'm too—'

'—clumsy,' they said at the same time.

'My God,' Jenny said quietly to Grace, 'he's Boy-Adie.'

'You!' a student prefect yelled. 'Clean that up, immediately, and get to the arena.'

The girls scrambled to help with the icky mess, Grace nearly gagging on the stench of the algae slime all over the floor.

3

bubble-running

The girls didn't catch Boy-Adie's name as they hurried to join the rest of the crowd surging towards the arena — an oval space the size of a football pitch — that seemed far too huge to be an open courtyard in the middle of the castle. He trotted ahead of them, tripping over himself in nervous haste to reach his seat, occasionally glancing back anxiously as if to urge them to move faster. He slotted into place with the rest of his team, waving at Adie as the girls passed by.

'Oh great,' Grace grumbled, spotting that the only remaining seats in the bleachers were again next to the Hawk Falls team. 'Think they'll get up as soon as we sit down?'

She sighed as the pixie-cut girl slapped her hand on the seat next to her and sneered, 'These seats are taken.'

Jenny grabbed Grace's arm, squeezed past others in the

row, and practically sat on pixie-cut's hand.

'Thanks,' she said, 'for holding them for us.'

Grace couldn't help grinning, and waved for the others to join them. The shrill voice of Lady Hecate rang out.

'Forget what training you've had. Forget who you know and what spells you've cast. It is all in the past. One thing only matters from here on out. One number.'

Standing on a scaffold built above the bleachers at one side of the arena, she snapped her fingers. Timber struts broke free of the structure, speeding to hover in the centre of the field, forming a long frame. Within the frame wooden letters appeared, like those on the wall of the Venetian Room, to form the names of every team.

Hawk Falls	0
Tempest Bridge	0
Radi Sky	0
Raven Hall	0
Balefire Warren	0

The list went on until, at the very bottom,

St John's of Dunbridge	-5

'Wait,' Rachel said, 'how come we're on minus five?'

There was a collective snicker from the girls in red uniform.

'That's what happens when idiot newbies don't know how to behave amongst their betters.'

Grace felt Jenny's body tense next to her, and knew something bad was coming.

'Listen, Blondie,' Jenny said.

'My name is Victoria Meister,' pixie-cut interrupted. 'You should remember it. It will be engraved on this year's trophy.'

'Look,' Grace said quickly, 'we're sorry if we got off on the wrong foot yesterday. This is all new to us, that's all. We didn't mean to upset anybody. Can't we start from scratch and be friends?'

She reached out her hand. Victoria smiled sweetly, and shook it.

'Ow!' Grace screamed, snapping into the back of her seat as the Hawk Falls team erupted in laughter.

'Surely even a witch-oag right out of the cradle knows what a Statica Ring is!' Victoria sneered.

Jenny grabbed Victoria's hand and snatched the ring from her finger, jumping a little with the same electric shock that had rushed through Grace. Victoria's dark eyes flashed beneath the short blonde hair, and Grace could feel a worrying surge of energy around them.

'Silence!' Lady Hecate's voice boomed. 'As I said, the only thing that matters from here on is one number.'

She looked pointedly to the Trial-board in the middle of the field. St John's had dipped another five points and Hawk

Falls, the name sliding all the way down to second-last place, had dropped to minus five. A gasp echoed around the arena, and Victoria Meister's eyes nearly fell out of her head.

'No!'

'Guess we're not so different after all, *Vicky*,' Jenny said, grinning.

'Jenny,' Grace whispered, 'don't push it.'

But there was no time for another argument as the field in front of them suddenly sank a couple of metres and then surged with muck, becoming more and more liquid until it was filled with water. Madame Three tottered to the edge of the scaffold and raised her hands.

'For your very first Trial, choose two members to compete in the Paired Bubble-Run Race. Let the Trials begin!'

The arena buzzed with excitement as the other teams began picking their two competitors.

'What the hell is bubble-running?' said Una.

'I read about it once,' Delilah replied. 'It's like flame-running, I think, but on water. You have to kick your feet back more so the water spins around you. If you get it right, you'll end up running inside a big bubble.'

'Right,' said Grace, 'it'll have to be you and Adie then. You guys ready?'

'But what are the rules?' Adie asked worriedly. 'Do we just run and that's it?'

'The others are lining up holding hands,' said Grace. 'What

do you think, Delilah? One big bubble?'

'Yes, I think so. That's going to be hard – we'll have to keep perfect time together.'

'On your marks,' Madame Three shrieked.

'Woah, they're starting already,' Jenny said, pushing Adie and Delilah towards the steps. 'Hurry.'

'I don't know,' Adie said, trying to turn back. 'I don't think I can do this.'

'You *have* to … I mean, of course you can. And give those Hawk harpies a good run for their money while you're at it.'

Grace gently took over, leading Adie down the steps as Delilah trotted ahead of them.

'Don't worry,' she said, 'we're not here to win, okay? We're just biding time 'til we can find a way out of here.'

That seemed to relax Adie a little, and she smiled. 'Okay. Just get through it, go through the motions.'

'That's it. Good luck.'

'Get set!' Madame Three's voice warbled with excitement.

Adie and Delilah levitated and pushed into their place in the line of pairs hovering just above the water.

'Go!'

A siren rang out in tune with Madame's Three's voice and there was a flurry of action. No-one moved forward at first, but dozens of feet pedalled madly, throwing growing waves of water behind them. Within a few seconds several teams had formed bubbles, but it was the Hawk Falls team that surged forward first. Victoria and a shorter red-haired team-mate ran in perfect time, rolling the bubble along the water like hamsters in a plastic ball. Adie and Delilah were already well behind the others. When they finally managed to form a bubble, Grace and Jenny let out an almighty squawk.

'Go Delilah! Go Adie!'

The two friends moved tentatively, looking a little wobbly as they tried to keep their feet in sync.

'Move it!' Jenny yelled, jumping on the spot. 'Come on, you can do it!'

'Take it easy,' Grace said. 'They're not trying to win, remember?'

'Why not? They're down there, they got themselves moving and … they're really picking up speed. Look at them go!'

Adie and Delilah had obviously found a rhythm, and were making steady progress. Despite her intentions, Grace found herself becoming caught up in the excitement.

'They're gonna pass out that lot,' Una said, punching the air. 'We won't be last!'

But the two girls in the bubble were even more ambitious. Grace could see Adie smiling as they passed another team, then another, and another.

'They're flying!' Rachel yelled over the cheering racket of the arena. 'We could win this!'

Jenny's boisterous applauding got louder and more urgent

as the St John's team raced on, getting closer and closer to the Hawk Falls bubble. They were now in fourth place and closing fast on the boys in third. Grace recognised one of them, with thick hair tied back, as the captain of Aura's team. The second boy was smaller in build, but able to keep up with his leader. Adie and Delilah skirted around the pair, but the boys swerved towards them in an effort to smash them into the wall enclosing the water.

'Hey!' Jenny shouted. 'Cheaters! Didn't anyone see that? Isn't there a referee?'

'Ha!' One of the more athletic of the Hawk Falls' girls snickered, and tossed her shock of wild hair, which was an unnatural shade of purple. 'You think you're at play-school? It's first over the finish line, idiot, no matter what. Get with the programme.'

'But they could really get hurt!'

Grace was talking to herself, but there was a cackle from the girls in red uniform and their purple-haired second-in-command.

'So what if they do? Will one of your teachers kiss the boo-boo and make it all better?'

Purple-hair had raised her voice deliberately, and laughter was spreading up the bleachers, but Grace was too worried to care. Her friends in the bubble had made it past Aura's team-mates, but only after another close call with the edge of the arena. The boy and girl in second place looked like twins – both tall and skinny with matching mops of raven-black hair – and although they didn't look powerful, they moved over the water with amazing speed and grace. They glanced back occasionally, keeping an eye on the approaching St John's team, and Grace hoped their more elegant style meant they'd be less aggressive.

She was wrong. As Adie and Delilah pulled up behind them, the Raven twins suddenly jumped in perfect unison, bouncing their bubble over the one behind. It rebounded on the St John's bubble, dunking it into the water, before bouncing ahead again. Adie and Delilah tipped forward, their hands gripping each other, trying to maintain their balance and speed as their bubble flipped back into the air and skidded across the surface of the fake lake, out of control.

'Oh no,' Una grabbed Grace's hand. 'They're going to crash into the wall!'

But the two girls were catching on quick. Delilah seemed to be giving fierce instructions as they sped towards the curved wall and, just in the nick of time, mimicking the Raven twins, she and Adie jumped in unison, bouncing backwards onto the track. Two more epic bounces forward, and they were in third place again. The Ravens zig-zagged in front, trying to block them overtaking, but the two girls slipped next to them, barely glancing off their bubble. The twins were off balance for a split second, but it was long enough for Adie and Delilah to sneak into second place.

'Woohoo!' Jenny was almost leaping into the next row with excitement. 'They're gonna win! Come on, Adie! Come on, Delilah! Move it! Just one more!'

It was infectious. Grace could feel her heart in her mouth as her friends closed the gap between them and Hawk Falls. She couldn't help herself.

'You can do it! Go Adie, go Delilah. You can do it!'

And then – a hiccup. Not even a hiccup. A momentary loss of concentration. Maybe they were tired, or nervous. Maybe it was just that they were inexperienced, but for a second Adie and Delilah lost their rhythm. They fell out of sync, their feet fumbling, their gaze fixed downwards as they tried to match up again. But at the speed they were going it was more than enough.

The bubble careened across the track, going even faster as they tripped and tumbled inside it, and smashed straight into Victoria Meister and her red-haired team-mate. Both bubbles burst in a halo of liquid, and four girls toppled into the murky water of the arena. Spluttering to the surface, Victoria leaned on Delilah's head, pushing the tiny girl under as she and her team-mate tried to struggle out of the lake. Adie and Delilah were narrowly missed by a speeding bubble, and all four girls were swallowed in its wake.

'They're going to drown!' Grace cried.

Jenny leapt into the next row and Grace followed, but they couldn't make it through the roaring crowds.

'Rachel!' Grace yelled. 'We can't get through. Can you fly down there?'

'I'm on it.'

Rachel took off into the air, graceful as ever, soaring towards her friends in the lake with arms outstretched, until she smacked into nothing and landed in a heap at the base of the bleachers. Dazed, she looked up at Grace.

'There's something there. Like a wall, but invisible. I can't get to them.'

'Cheating,' Madame Three's voice echoed through the air, 'will not be tolerated.'

The raven-haired twins had crossed the finish line and the Trial-board above the arena was fluttering again, but all Grace could see were the flailing limbs of her friends, trapped like bumpers in a giant pinball machine.

The water was suddenly sucked from the edges of the arena, rising in the centre to form two seats, one holding Adie, the other Delilah. With a sweep of her hand, Adie raised another two, rescuing Victoria Meister and her red-haired partner. The remaining teams finished the race as the watery chairs travelled to one side, depositing the girls safely on the edge. Grace heaved a sigh of relief, remembering the feeling of being pulled from the river back home by one of Adie's watery creations. Her friend really did have a flair for that kind of thing.

Grace raced down to meet her soaking friends and hugged

them tight. She did not miss the look of pure venom from Victoria. The Trial-board had settled and St John's were now at minus fifteen. Hawk Falls was still in second last place, with minus five. Grace felt a growing knot of dread in her stomach. There was something about Victoria's glare that sent shivers up her spine. The Trials were dangerous already, and she now had no doubt that vengeance would come from Hawk Falls. She had to find a way to get her friends out of this strange and frightening world, and back home where they belonged.

4

THE CLOSET

'No boats!' Delilah exclaimed. 'No boats, please. At least …
let's just walk for a bit.'

Grace couldn't blame her. She and Adie were still sopping
wet, and it wasn't as if the gondolas would take them to the
cosy warmth of a real fire and fluffy blankets. There wasn't
even a change of clothes in their cold Venetian Room.

'We've got to find you guys some dry clothes. Come to
think of it, none of us has a spare pair of anything. It was
alright for one night, but pretty soon–'

'We're going to start ponging up the place.' Jenny pulled
back the collar of her jumper and sniffed under her arm.
'Not quite there yet.'

'Nice.'

'And I've got no makeup, either,' Rachel said, tapping her

cheeks as if to rouge them with her fingertips.

'Why don't you use a little glamour spell?'

'I am!'

'Oh. Then use a little more.'

Rachel shot her a look, but Grace was distracted by the *Library* sign above a pair of mahogany doors. It suddenly hit her – if they were going to find a way out of this supernatural world, they were going to need some supernatural information. She veered towards the doors, but was abruptly accosted by a boy who barely came up to her shoulder, with thick milk-bottle glasses and a slight overbite. His quivering hands held a well-used notebook and pencil, though his jittery demeanor seemed more like excitement than nervousness. By his right hand was a girl even shorter than him. Her round face was freckled and pleasant, and she looked up at Grace from under a halo of sandy ringlets with an expectant smile.

'Eder Verzerrt, *The Lyceum Gazette*.' The boy took Grace's hand and shook it earnestly.

'Uh, Grace Brennan–'

'St John's of Dunbridge,' Eder interrupted. 'And this is Una, Rachel, Jenny – the rebel without a cause – and, of course, the two stars of the Bubble-Running battle.' He solemnly shook hands with Adie and Delilah.

'I'm sorry,' said Grace. 'Have we met?'

'We are meeting,' Eder replied cheerfully. 'And it is a pleasure.'

'But you know our names already.'

'Lyceum lists of registration.' He tapped his head with the pencil. 'Know it off by heart.'

'Registration? I didn't know we—'

'Must stay ahead of the competition. Breaking news is only breaking news when it is breaking. After that, it's broke.'

'Uh-huh.'

'So I'm looking for the inside scoop on the team that has set tongues wagging and ignited the fury of the defending champions; the ones who have defied convention and tried to cheat their way through the very first trial, risking disqualification and eternity in the dungeons.'

'Eternal what?' Una gulped.

'You know,' Eder whispered behind his hand, 'no-one has ever come out. They go in, they don't come out. But *you*! You laugh in the face of disqualification, and cheat anyway. Such defiance!'

'That was an accident,' Adie cut in. 'We were just trying not to drown and—'

But Eder continued with his jittery zeal.

'So I and my learned colleague, Peach,' he indicated the round-faced girl, whose smile broadened, 'will be following your exploits with ardent fervour. And may I say that not for many years has there been such exquisite disruption as— b-bee-beep, b-bee-bee-beep, beep-beep, b-bee-bee-beep.'

Grace stepped back with fright. Eder Verzerrt's head was

twitching to one side and he was making disturbing sounds like Morse code.

'Incoming,' said Peach brightly.

'What?' said Grace.

'Breaking news,' the girl replied. 'He gets it all.'

'How do you mean? He … he's getting messages?'

'Conscientia spell, two years ago. To receive all breaking news. And so he does.'

'All the time? He can't switch it off?'

'Wouldn't want to if he could.' Peach grinned. 'One finger always on the pulse.'

'B-bee-beep, b-b-bee-beep,' said Eder.

Grace shifted her feet uncomfortably.

'So, do we just ignore it?' Jenny asked.

'Speak to me in the meantime,' replied Peach, still smiling. 'He knows what I know.'

'Beep.' Eder suddenly stopped twitching. '– as your wonderful display this morning. May I congratulate you, and urge you to continue this newsworthy venture.'

He shook all of their hands again before turning and leaving, with Peach perfectly in step beside him.

'So. Disqualification,' Jenny said. 'Let's not do that then.'

'Yeah,' replied Grace. 'That doesn't sound good.'

'I think we made a friend there,' said Una, smiling.

'How can you tell?'

'Well, he didn't point and laugh, call us idiots *or* try to drown any of us. Peach. Is that a real name? Or Eder?'

'Doesn't matter. It's library time.'

Grace marched towards the heavy double doors and pushed them hard. They opened straight into the young girl from the dining room, who had bumped into Adie at breakfast. She had been standing behind the doors, holding a huge pile of black slate pieces, each about the size of a book, which clattered to the ground.

'Ooh, I'm so sorry,' Grace said, stooping to pick them up. 'It's Aura, isn't it?'

'Yes,' the girl smiled. 'And don't worry about these, they don't break or anything.'

'What are they for?' Adie asked, picking up a black shard that had skidded across the polished floorboards.

'They're home slates.'

'Sorry?'

'*Home* slates,' Aura replied, as if it was obvious. 'Here take some.' She handed one to each of them. 'I was bringing back some for the team, but I can get more. You can borrow a dozen if you've got a library card.'

'What do they do?' asked Rachel.

Aura giggled as if it was a silly question.

'Home slates, for watching people back home. You know, when you're homesick. Do you call them something else?'

'Eh, I guess so,' Grace said, wiping her hand over the dull, black stone.

Aura giggled again, and shook her head. 'Bad luck today. It was very close.'

'A little too close,' said Adie.

'And cold,' Delilah said. 'I wish we had some dry clothes.'

'Why don't you get some from the Closet?' said Aura.

'Can we?' said Adie. 'I mean … we were going to but, we weren't sure where it was.'

'Oh, I can show you, no problem. It's on the way to my room anyway. Come with me.'

The girls followed as Aura skipped ahead of them, her bantu knots bobbing in the air as she trotted with a happy step.

'You guys go ahead,' Grace said, turning back to the open double doors. 'I'm going to check out the library to see if we can— em, to look up … you know, something. I'll catch up with you later.'

'Will you be able to find your way back?' Delilah asked.

'If I get lost I'll just hop on a gondola.'

Rachel smoothed the creases of the sky-blue dress, her eyes widening as the light caught the gold flecks in the deep blue stones embroidered into the material. It fit perfectly. She turned left and right, loving how tall the dress made her look, and bemoaning her lack of makeup. It was fine to use a bit of glamour when there was nothing else to hand, but she had to be aware of it all the time. If she relaxed and forgot about it the glamour faded, leaving her eyes un-lined and smaller-looking with, she imagined, the hint of bags underneath. She had her grandmother's eyes. She'd give them back if she could.

'Can I take this?'

'You can take anything you want!' Aura chimed. 'It's the Closet. You just– Oh, you don't want to take that though, do you? You couldn't wear it.'

'Holy moly, Rach,' said Una, pulling up the brim of a scarlet sombrero to get a good look, 'you look like a movie star.'

Rachel shrugged, but smiled.

'You really do look pretty in blue,' said Adie.

'You can't run in that get-up,' Jenny snapped, hopping up and down as she pulled on a pair of buckled ankle boots. 'Get something practical. There won't be any need for cocktail dresses around here.'

'How do you know?' Rachel said, swinging the long flared skirts and watching them shimmer.

'Knock it off and pick out some proper clothes or we'll be here all day. You've gotta get some pjs as well, don't forget.'

'And your unmentionables,' said Una.

'Underwear, Una, just say underwear. And you can quit with the dressing up too. You don't need a sombrero.'

Una removed the hat and flung it like a frisbee onto the giant revolving hatstand that took up one corner of the open space that was the Closet.

Rachel was taking one last glance at herself in the mirror when she felt a tugging at the zip. Aura seemed in a hurry to return the dress to one of the many conveyor belts that moved like an army of millipedes stacked against the walls, their thousands of legs composed of hanging clothes of every description.

'Do you think I could hang on to this?' Rachel asked quietly, slipping the dress off and keeping one eye on Jenny to make sure she couldn't hear.

'You couldn't wear it,' Aura replied.

'Oh, I know I probably wouldn't have any parties to wear it to here, but I like it so much.' She handed the dress over and pulled her boring old school jumper on over her head. 'I'd just try it on in our room sometimes and, you never know, maybe there will be some party–'

'You really couldn't wear it!' the girl replied in earnest as she stuffed the dress under a plastic cover on the hanger. 'All that blue goldstone? It's a faery magnet!' The worried crease between Aura's eyebrows disappeared once the dress was safely stowed on a crawling conveyor belt, and her bright eyes were cheery once more. 'I can't believe you even tried it on in here. You're so brave! Those faeries…'

'Faeries? You mean, like, *faeries*? With wings? They're real?'

Aura rolled her eyes and swatted her hand gently, as if Rachel was playing dumb with her.

'They're *everywhere* here,' she whispered conspiratorially. 'Hy-Breasal is Faery Land, we're surrounded by them. Not in the castle grounds though, they can't come in here. Too afraid.'

'Are they dangerous?'

'The *most* dangerous.' Aura hunched her shoulders, grinning, like someone about to tell the scariest ghost story around the camp fire. 'Nowhere has faeries as wicked and gross as Hy-Breasal. If they find a witch-oag in a cradle, they'll steal it and replace it with one of theirs that's sickly. And if one catches you in the woods, it'll take the form of a horse or bull and trample you to pieces. Or the really nasty ones will bewitch you with phantom lights and lead you off the edge of a cliff!'

'That *is* scary.'

'Someday,' Aura went on, snatching a cape from a passing hanger and swinging it dramatically over her shoulders, 'I'll be a Hunter, and I'll chase down the faeries and rid Hy-Breasal of Every. Last. One. Hah!'

She lashed out with an invisible sword, swinging again in triumph as she hit her target.

'Oh, okay,' Rachel said. 'So, we should stay inside the castle grounds then?'

'Inside the castle walls,' Aura said solemnly, raising her sword, 'where I can protect you.'

She swung again, and another imaginary faery was struck down.

'You got your stuff picked out, Rach?'

Jenny stood by the door in the buckled ankle boots, ready to leave. Rachel quickly appraised her friend's outfit and despaired a little. She admired Jenny's rebellious flair, but the loose-fitting t-shirt and studded belt was drifting too far from deliberate-grunge into accidental-heavy-metal.

The trick to dressing like you don't care what people think, is to really care what people think, Rachel said to herself. Out loud, she said, 'Haven't got everything yet.'

'Has anyone seen Delilah?' Adie asked. 'She ran in between those racks when we got here and I haven't seen her since.'

'I'll find her,' Rachel said, 'and we'll follow you out when we're ready.'

'Alright. Aura, you mind showing us back to the canal?' said Jenny.

'No problem!' The young girl kept the cape on as she skipped to the door, making it billow out behind her like a superhero.

'Don't forget a couple of jumpers,' Jenny said to Rachel over her shoulder. 'You'll need them.'

'And your unmentionables,' Una said primly as she disappeared into the corridor.

'*Underwear,* Una, jeez.' Jenny's voice drifted away and Rachel was left with just the harmonic hum of the conveyor belts and the swish of plastic-covered clothes.

She collected garments until she couldn't carry any more. With a tall stack of neatly folded jeans, tops, and one truly hideous Victorian-looking nightdress (the others had taken the only decent-looking pyjamas), she went looking for Delilah amongst the groaning racks.

She eventually found her gazing at her reflection in a mirror, and wearing grey shapeless trousers, a buttoned shirt and a maroon jumper.

'Delilah, is that what you picked out?' Rachel deposited her collection of clothes on the floor, and glanced at the pile of clothes at Delilah's feet, seeing more shapeless trousers, jumpers and plain tops. 'That's pretty much our school uniform. Don't you want to pick out some stuff you like?'

'I like this.'

Delilah stared at her reflection, her head tilted so her wavy, black hair shadowed her face. Rachel glanced again at the sad pile of clothes. She wondered if Mrs Quinlan had ever taken Delilah shopping, now that the small girl lived with her. And before that, had her mother, Ms Gold, ever bothered?

Ms Meredith Gold had outwardly been the most beautiful person Rachel had ever seen. But underneath her honey-coloured locks and luminous skin beat a heart as black as coal. The girls had never asked Delilah what life had been like with her mother, and Rachel wouldn't ask now.

'You know, if you're not sure what suits you, I can help you with that.'

With sudden inspiration, Rachel began snatching tops and jeans, throwing them in Delilah's direction.

'You want to go for high-waisted jeans and trousers,' she said in a flurry of hangers and protective plastic, 'so you're not cut in half. That'll make you look taller. And v-necks are great for petite shapes. And monochrome, no mad patterns or too many colours on your frame. You want to keep it simple. And *shoes*.'

She ran off to the shoe section, shouting as she ran her finger along the rows of perfectly placed pairs, finding soft leather sling-backs that she had to stop herself adding to her own collection.

'Can you wear heels? Are you allowed? It's the one thing my mum won't budge on. I can get away with two inches on special occasions and, I mean, I have hidden a pair in my bag sometimes so I can change when I'm out. But my mum's convinced that heels are the devil.' She jogged back and knelt in front of Delilah, holding out a sparkly sandal like Prince Charming for Cinderella. 'I'm not allowed to wear them until my feet stop growing. She says I could get bunions, or in-growing toenails, but I don't know. I think that might be a load of rubbish.'

She didn't notice anything was wrong until Delilah suddenly backed away.

'No. I like this.'

'But ... don't you want–'

'I like this.'

Rachel realised she'd pushed too hard. The withdrawn

expression on Delilah's face was the same as when Meredith was still around, before she'd been thrown down the demon well and Delilah taken into the care of Mrs Quinlan. But she had begun to change in the last few months, from a quiet thing that barely spoke to a bright young girl with strong opinions and obvious talent. With Adie, it seemed, she had formed a special bond, and her gift for magic flourished when they worked together.

But it was a fragile new beginning and, all too often, something would shut down inside and Delilah would become the compliant, quiet girl from before. Rachel looked up into the big, brown eyes and knew the shell had closed around her friend once again.

'Okay,' she said, placing the pile of lonely, grey clothes in Delilah's arms. 'We'll take these then.'

5

in a cold, dark corner

Grace's fingers traced the gold letters stamped on the cloth-bound spines. *Practical Applications of the Four Leaf Clover; Merrows and the Curse of the Mermaid's Call; The Leanan-Sidhe and other Vampires*.

She would never say it to the girls, because she would sound even nerdier than usual, but she loved the smell of books. There was something old and earthy in the scent of a library and in this one, where every book seemed at least a hundred years old, it was like exploring deep inside the folds of the Earth.

At first the library hadn't seemed any more magical than her local library at home but, as she moved from one section to the next, opening and scanning dozens of books, she felt the atmosphere, and her mood, change. Faery lore, under various names, seemed to dominate in most subjects. Most mythical creatures in this world were actually faeries of different forms, and scaring them off, blocking their attacks or getting rid of them in general was the most covered topic.

She replaced a red-covered edition of *The Gwyllion Stare: The Unknown Truth*, and turned a corner into an aisle that seemed full of sunlight. She felt instantly warmer, happier and surrounded by nature, like the shelves were trees in full blossom, and the carpet beneath her feet was soft, green grass. The books around her looked fresh and new, regardless of age, and were all about flora and fauna, and the importance of the Wiccan's relationship with nature. She turned another corner, and was hit with a blast of cold wind. The briny scent of seaweed permeated the air, and an impossible gale whistled through the stacks. Here, the shelves were full of stories about the sea, witches controlling water, and hideous creatures that dragged ships to their doom at the bottom of the ocean.

Time flew by as Grace strolled in and out of different sections, her moods swinging as she felt gleeful one minute, pensive the next, drifting through this ultimate of libraries. But as she neared the back of the room, something cold crept over her. It wasn't just the temperature dropping, but the sensation of icy fingers inching their way up her back. The light dimmed until she had trouble seeing in front of her, and her shoes squelched in the carpet that appeared to be rotting beneath her feet. In the gloom she could see the speckled black of mould reaching up the walls, and the maggot-ridden shelves held books that were warped and disintegrating with damp. She scanned the grimy-looking titles: *Wickedness and the Human Fallacy; From Afar: A Study in Human Weakness; Homo Sapiens: The Wiccan Neanderthal.*

She felt like she was shrinking, like her body was actually getting smaller and smaller under the threatening, close air that stank of rot and hate. She leaned hard on the shelves for support, ignoring the squishing maggots beneath her fingertips, and longed for home; one tiny glimpse of something familiar that would alleviate this horrible darkness.

Crrrreakk.

The shelf bent under her hand and suddenly snapped in two, spilling its contents onto the squelchy carpet. A green-covered book, entitled *Between the Wiccan and the Human World,* landed right at her feet. Grace dropped to her knees, and flipped it open. The book was full of spidery text and intricate maps. She flipped back and read down the contents until she got to number eleven, *Crossing the Water: The Ferryman.* She rifled through to the right page and started reading.

✱ ✱ ✱

'Rachel said that we're on this island, Hy-Breasal, right? Well then, it's this Ferryman that can travel between the two worlds, this and ours.' Back in the Venetian Room, Grace pointed to the text that described the Ferryman and how to find him. 'This, people, is how we get home!'

'It says here we've to pay him,' Jenny said. 'How much does it cost? And do you think he's going to take *euros*?'

'I've seven euros and thirty cents,' Una said, digging through her pockets and finding another coin. 'Thiry-*five* cents.'

'I don't think he'll take euros, Una,' Grace said, carefully turning the decaying pages.

'Looks to me like this is one of those *It'll cost you your soul* kind of deals.' Jenny was tucking her newly acquired wardrobe into the one of the stone alcoves. 'We're not signing a blank cheque to get on some dodgy ferry.'

'But this could be our way home.'

'Or our way into a dungeon with some supernatural creep. Not a chance, Grace. We'll have to find another way.'

'What if there *is* no other way?'

'Of course there'll be another way. There'll be a spell we can do, or some transporting potion, something we can do ourselves without trusting some ancient weirdo we've never met. I'm not taking that chance.'

'It's not only up to you!'

'Fine, then we'll take a vote.'

Grace looked around the room and knew there was no point. No-one liked the idea. Adie was avoiding her gaze, like she did whenever she didn't want to disagree out loud; Rachel didn't seem in any mad rush to leave as she sorted through her alcove full of new clothes; and Delilah was hiding behind her hair, the way she did whenever she became withdrawn and frightened. She'd go with whoever talked the loudest. And Jenny could talk loud.

'It's cold here, and I can't sleep, and everything's scary,' Una said firmly. 'I want to get a lift with this Ferryman.'

Grace dropped the book to the floor and climbed into her half-hammock in the canal.

'Doesn't matter, Una. No-one else does.'

✳ ✳ ✳

Unable to sleep, Grace tapped her fingernails on the black slate that Aura had given her. A *home* slate, she had called it, a way to see your friends and family when you were home-sick. But Grace didn't know how to make it work. She lay in her half-hammock, curled around the shard of black stone, listening to the almost-snores of Adie and the definite-snores of Jenny. She missed her own bed, and her mum's cooking, and her own clothes. She even missed getting up for school in the morning. But most of all she missed her mum. There was only the two of them, and it grieved Grace to think of what her mum must be going through.

Would time pass at the same rate here? Would everyone at home know they were missing? Were Ms Lemon and Mrs Quinlan worried sick, and trying to reach them? She curled tighter into the sackcloth that bobbed on the water, and a single tear rolled down her cheek and dropped onto the slate.

Out of the blackness appeared a flurry of light.

Grace sat bolt upright as an image focused on the stone like a flatscreen tv. Her mother sat at their kitchen table, opposite a Garda scribbling on a little notepad. There was no sound, but Patricia Brennan was talking a mile a minute between hiccuping sobs, clutching a tattered tissue in one hand. Her eyes were swollen. She had obviously been crying for hours. The Garda was nodding sympathetically, patting her mother's hand but, though her mother kept on talking, he had stopped writing. Eventually, Mrs Brennan's sobs took over and she covered her face with her hands.

Grace watched for as long as she could bear it then, with tears streaming down her own face, she covered the image with her palm. The light faded and the slate turned black. She buried her sobs in the crook of her elbow, trying not to wake the others. But sniffling above her told her someone was already awake.

'Una?'

Grace looked over the ledge at the silhouette lying in a cold alcove. There was a faint light that quickly faded, and the clatter of slate on stone.

'Una, are you okay?'

There was no answer, but the sniffling stopped abruptly. Grace could make out the shape of shuddering shoulders in the dark, and her heart ached even more.

'I'll get us home, Una. Soon. I promise.'

In the silence of the night, Grace decided what had to be done. And with the comfort of certainty, she finally fell asleep.

✳ ✳ ✳

'Glamour,' Madame Three barked from the centre of the arena, 'is the blade of the Wiccan sword. A terrible beauty, a cruel allure, and the flame in the torch of every Hunter… Time and beauty … Beauty and time … You see?'

She trailed off, seeming to lose her train of thought, and paced in a tight circle. Grace could get a closer look at the woman from the front row this time. The bleachers had moved from outside the barriers of the arena, to the inside, and Madame Three was only a few metres away. The swathes of velvet that cloaked her stout body dragged over the dry muck of the arena, and her blonde hair clung to her head in tight curls. Her skin was smooth and plump, but there was something not quite right about her face. It was as if the muscles beneath were desperate to sag, but were held reluctantly aloft with invisible scaffolding. Grace felt weary as she watched the woman pace around the table that stood in the centre of the bleachers, and wished that one of the other Supremes would intercede to move things along. But Lord Machlau's gaze was firmly aimed at the ground, and Lady

Hecate's thin lips were pursed with severity.

'Glamour!' Madame Three suddenly exclaimed, pointing at a birdcage on the table, which held a tiny creature. 'Win the wood nymph's trust, and he shall take your hand. And your glory shall grow.'

She indicated the Trial-board that hung in the air above them, as Lady Hecate finally stepped forward.

'Competitors must use their glamour skills to entice the wood nymph from the cage, and remember, not every faery is as enticing as the next. Choose your breed well.'

A boy from Raven Hall was first to compete. He swept his long-fingered hands over his face, and his glamour spell revealed a shrivelled frame, with a blunt face and pointed ears. He had so little flesh that his ribs protruded over his concave stomach. He opened the door of the birdcage and poked his bony fingers through, wriggling them like worms on a hook. But the nymph remained pressed against the bars opposite, and refused to move.

After several minutes Lady Hecate shrieked 'A highland brownie. Fail!'

The next competitors stepped up and tried their glamour spells on the wood nymph.

'A fir darrig. Fail!'

'A bogle. Fail!'

There were varying degrees of failure. Sometimes the nymph would trot around the waiting fingers, even nipping at those that poked too hard, and other times he remained at the back of the cage and watched with suspicion.

At last a slender girl from Hawk Falls approached the cage. Her faery mimicked her own figure, long and graceful, with delicate wings that stretched from far above her head to the ground, glinting like frosted glass. Long tresses of golden hair cloaked her like a cape and, instead of jabbing her fingers into the cage, she knelt down and whispered inaudibly. After a short while the wood nymph crept forward, eventually leaving the safety of the cage. The girl snatched the tiny creature and held him, squealing, in the air, as her glamour faded. The Hawk Falls team leapt to their feet in triumph, and Grace caught the self-satisfied smirk of captain Victoria Meister.

'Success for Hawk Falls!' called Lady Hecate and then, with a grimace, 'and now for our final team. St John's of Dunbridge, please choose your competitor.'

'That's a no-brainer,' said Una, giving Rachel a slap on the back.

'Maybe try and copy the Hawk Falls girl,' Grace said, before catching herself. 'But you know it doesn't matter. We're not here to win.'

'Right,' said Rachel, winking at Jenny as she made her way to the table.

Grace couldn't help it, her heart was fluttering in her chest. She held her breath as Rachel stood, for what seemed like forever, in front of the table, breathing slowly and pre-paring herself. Finally, as some tutting and moaning echoed around the arena, she finally lifted her hands to her face, and *disappeared*.

'Holy fudgeballs!' Una shrieked. 'She's *gone*!'

'Where?' Adie said. 'Where did she go? Oh God!'

Grace felt panic rise in her throat like bile, until she saw the tiny figure on the table open the door of the cage from the outside.

Rachel tried to block out the stares of the entire arena. She could feel them watching her back, just like she could feel the gaze of a tall man who stood at the entrance of the stadium, hidden between the bleachers. She had noticed him about halfway through the Trial, and couldn't keep her eyes off him. His skin was so dark it had a hint of blue, but his eyes were pale, like tiny moons. His shaved head made his features look even more chiselled, and his clothes ... his *clothes*. He was dressed like a privateer – one of those action heroes from olden times, who fought battles on the high seas – in a form-fitting leather jerkin, topped with a ruffled collar, right under his chin. His breeches and boots matched, and a sword and jewelled scabbard hung from his waist.

He was focussed entirely on the competitors, and appeared to ignore everything else that was going on in the arena. As

Rachel had taken her place at the table, she knew his focus would now be on her. But she tried to block it out, that and all the other distractions that came from the waiting crowd. She had never before attempted what she was about to do. She had reduced her size in glamour once or twice in the past, but not by much. It would take every ounce of concentration she had. Feeling the buzz in her fingertips, she built it up slowly, letting it grow until it was so fierce it reverberated through every cell of her body. Finally, when she couldn't hold on to it anymore, she rippled her fingers over her face and the world dropped away.

When she opened her eyes she was standing on the table, outside the birdcage, and the little wood nymph was eyeing her with curiosity.

6

THE HUNTERS' mansion

The wood nymph trotted back and forth across the cage, swinging out of the bars, like an excited toddler in a playground, always with his eyes on Rachel. She waited patiently outside, startling a little when he leapt suddenly onto the bars above her. The glamour was a façade – she wasn't really small enough to stand on the table, and she couldn't fit through the tiny door – but the magic made her seem small to the world, and made the world seem huge to her.

Hanging upside down, the wood nymph stuck his finger between his lips and shook it, making a *b-burr b-burr b-burr* sound. Rachel giggled. The nymph seemed pleased he had made her laugh, and grinned, repeating the sound. When she laughed again, he reached out and gently *booped* her nose with one gnarled finger. She raised her hand and he leaned through the door, so she could touch his nose. His skin felt grainy, like rough tissue paper, and he smelled like the woods. Swinging right side up, he dropped to the threshold of the door.

Rachel saw her chance and stepped backwards, holding out her hands. After a moment, the nymph smiled, came towards her and grabbed both her hands, spinning her around the table in a lively jig. Rachel squealed with delight as noise erupted all around them. At last, when she was out of breath, she touched the nymph gently on the nose again.

'Thank you for the dance. Bye bye, little man.'

The full-sized world rushed back with dizzying speed, and she had to lean on the table as her knees went weak. The wood nymph shrieked in terror at the giant girl looming over him, and scurried back inside the cage.

Rachel was dismayed. 'Oh no! Hey, sorry, little man, I didn't mean to—'

But she was interrupted by Jenny's athletic frame landing on her from behind.

'Rach, you're a freaking genius!'

Jenny's iron grip almost choked the life out of her, but she laughed as the other girls all tried to hug her at the same time.

'We're only five points behind those Hawk Falls wenches

now.' Jenny had roughly turned her to face the reddening complexion of Victoria Meister.

'Cheat,' the pixie-cut girl said, marching towards them.

'Yeah?' Jenny said combatively. 'How'd she cheat?'

'I don't know,' Victoria replied, '*yet*. But you cheated in the last Trial, and no-one without Hunter training could glamour a *wood nymph*.'

'Well, she did. So suck it up, loser.'

'Jenny.' Rachel heard the warning in Grace's voice and followed her gaze to Victoria's hands, which hung by her side, crackling with some sort of fierce energy.

'I think it's time the newbies were taught a lesson.' The crackling energy was now climbing up Victoria's arms.

'Bring it on, sweetie,' Jenny said, releasing her grip on Rachel, 'but there ain't nothing you can teach me.'

'SILENCE.'

The buzz of the arena muted instantly, and everyone turned to face Lady Hecate, who stood high on the bleachers, with the handsome privateer behind her.

'The victor of today's Trial has been summoned by the Hunters.' There was a hushed gasp throughout the crowd. 'St John's of Dunbridge, you will relinquish your competitor for the remainder of the day.'

The hordes of students separated silently, making a path from Rachel to the bleachers. She shook her head.

'Grace,' she whispered, 'do you think it's safe?'

'I don't know.'

In the immediate crowd she saw a shock of strawberry blond hair and a very wide smile. Boy-Adie was waving his arms in encouragement. 'Go!' he said, grinning.

'What's going to happen to her? Will she be okay?' Adie asked.

Boy-Adie's lanky frame shook with barely contained excitement.

'She'll get to see the Hunters' Mansion. It's a great honour!'

Adie was still eyeing her with worry, but Rachel's mind was set at ease. Her echoing footsteps were the only sound as she waved at her friends and made her way through the crowd and up onto the bleachers.

'This is Aruj of Morgane,' Lady Hecate said, her expression showing no pleasure in making the introduction.

'You have a gift, Rachel of Dunbridge.' Aruj's voice was low and deep, like a sound from the depths of the ocean.

Rachel couldn't reply. The pale eyes set in dark skin were striking, almost hypnotic. With considerable effort she finally managed a smile, and followed close behind him as he led her out of the arena.

✳ ✳ ✳

'I hope she'll be alright.' Grace watched her friend leave with the stranger in the weird outfit, and tried not to worry.

'I'm sure it's fine,' Una said lightly. 'They probably won't torture her for information or anything.'

'*Una.*'

'I said they probably *won't.*'

Grace sighed.

'Jenny's still itching for a fight, I can tell.'

'Yeah, she's got that snorting bull look she gets sometimes. Never seen her actually fight anyone, though. I mean, like, with fists. Do you think she would?'

'Sometimes I wonder.'

'Hey,' Una said, nudging her in the ribs, 'take a look at Adie and Boy-Adie. I don't know who's gone redder.'

Grace grinned as Adie chatted with an embarrassed smile, and the tall boy jammed his hands self-consciously into his pockets. Una nudged her again.

'Delilah's gone to the dark side, though. Look, she's practically hiding under those bleachers.'

'Don't say it like that, Una.'

'I don't mean it in a bad way. I just mean she's doing that thing again, where she goes all quiet. Like she was before …'

Adie came skipping towards them, saving them the unpleasantness of having to remember Delilah's mother.

'Hey, you guys. Want to head inside for dinner?'

'So,' said Una, 'did you finally get his name?'

'His name's Gaukroger,' Adie replied.

'Oh, I'm so sorry.'

'I like Gaukroger.'

'I like him too, but that's a terrible name.'

✳ ✳ ✳

Rachel tried to keep her eyes open as the barren land sped past. She wanted to take in as much of this new world as she could, but she was still adjusting to the green hue that saturated everything, as if the whole of Hy-Breasal was radioactive.

She was sailing on land, on a ship with big, graceful sails, which gouged a deep groove in the ground as it moved. It was piloted by Aruj in all his swash-buckling glory. She held fast to the side; it was a bit much that just the two of them were travelling on this huge ship that could hold a hundred people – Grace would undoubtedly have something to say about their carbon footprint. But Rachel had no idea if witchcraft added to the greenhouse effect, or even if it *could* be wasted. Besides, the thrill was worth it.

Aruj had barely spoken since their introduction. He was a man of few words, which meant that he was probably really deep and mysterious. She made a bet with herself that he had a very tragic past too. He might have lost the love of his life at sea, or fallen for a mermaid, but they could never be together because they came from two different worlds. Or something. She sighed and forced her eyelids apart again, straining against the perpetual green.

The Hunters' Mansion lived up to the promise of Aruj's

outfit. It was palatial, with the main part of the building flanked by two taller wings. Rachel didn't know exactly what *gothic* was, but she was sure this house must be it, with its dark grey stone, tall narrow windows, and pointy mouldings at the top, like someone had painted the mansion then held it upside down so the paint ran. The grounds were large enough to house the ship inside its high walls, and the gardens were full of grey and silver flowering bushes. Yes, this place was definitely *gothic*.

Aruj led her through the wrought-iron doors into the entrance hall, dark and grand with polished wood and a wide staircase that split in two at the landing, leading left and right further into the house. There were oil paintings in ornate brass frames, portraits of elegant women and handsome men, all dressed as if prepared for battle.

'Rachel of Dunbridge,' Aruj's depths-of-the-ocean voice said, 'meet Alinda of Morgane.'

Confused, Rachel turned to face an extraordinarily beautiful woman who seemed to have materialised out of nowhere. Her eyes were pale, like Aruj's, but her skin was also pale. She wore breeches and boots like those of Rachel's privateer guide, but on top she wore a loose blouse, enclosed by a leather corset that pinched her waist to an impossibly small size. Though she looked to be in her twenties, her hair was fully silver, and swept back in an up-style of relaxed braids and twists; the kind of boho chic look that Rachel had yet to master. She wondered how long those tresses of silver hair would be if let down. Rachel had once had a mild cardiac event when she found a grey hair hidden in her sleek, dark locks but if premature ageing made you look anything like Alinda, she'd be quite happy.

'Welcome, Rachel of Dunbridge.' Alinda's smile was epic.

'Just ... Rachel is fine. It's so nice to meet you. This place is gorgeous, really, it's so fancy. I love all the old pictures and stuff. They must be really ancient.'

Alinda and Aruj smiled in reply, the way deep, mysterious people do. Rachel wished she could shut her own babbling mouth. It was so uncool.

'Let me show you what you're here to see.' Alinda moved like she was on a travelator; her head didn't bob up and down when she walked and, try as she might, Rachel couldn't imitate it without losing her balance. So she resorted to her own stupid, clunky walk and followed the silver-haired woman up the stairs, with Aruj close behind.

✧ ✧ ✧

The decor remained dark and stately throughout the main part of the house, but when they moved into the west wing, the rooms took Rachel's breath away. They entered via a pillared gallery, with a curved ceiling that was painted with colourful and detailed hunting scenes. Gold mouldings decorated the buttresses and balconies and, peering over the mezzanine, she could see the marble floor beneath, soft in colour and polished like glass. She'd been on holiday to France one summer, and this place reminded her of the Palace of Versailles. When she got back everyone had asked her if she'd been to the Eiffel Tower. She had, but she couldn't think why anyone cared about *that*. Versailles was full of lavish rooms, gold paint and expensive stuff. Marie Antoinette had lived there (she couldn't remember which century) and she had thrown the most awesome parties. She had been married to the King and was the ultimate fashionista but, for some reason, everyone hated her and in the end she got her head chopped off.

At the end of the gallery they moved into another gorgeous hall. There were doors on each side, some of them open, and Rachel glimpsed more luscious decoration. Each room had its own colour palette and distinctive style. One had furnishings in mint green, with rounded feet on the tables and chairs. Another was deep crimson, decadent and vicious, with dagger-shaped ends on the curtain rails and fireguards. Her guides led her up the wide staircase, past a gold-plated suit of armour and shining old-fashioned weapons displayed on the walls.

'I'd love to see inside that yellow room.' Rachel couldn't help herself blurting, as she passed yet another sumptuous chamber. 'I don't think I've seen so much silk in all my life.'

'These aren't the rooms you wish to see,' said Aruj. '*These*

75

are the rooms you wish to see.'

Alinda pushed open a door at what Rachel was certain had been the end of the building. She caught glimpses out of the windows on the landing, and was sure there was nothing but the gardens beyond. But they stepped into a tunnel that seemed to have been dug out of this world and into the earth of another. Primitive torches lined walls that were nothing more than rough clay, the same clay that was soft beneath their feet. In the poor light, Rachel followed Alinda's graceful steps until the woman stopped at a door on the right side. She gestured at a window in the door, and Rachel looked in.

A handsome man, also dressed as a privateer, stood in the large, clay room, his shirt sleeves pushed up to his elbows, and a long sword in his right hand. With a shock she noticed the hideous creature that lurked by the far wall. Its nose was long and curved, its skin the colour of a scummy pond. The hair that sprouted from its misshapen head was like dry grass, and on the end of its scrawny arms were overly long, knobby fingers. It hissed with malice at the man, lashing out with its knarled hands, but the privateer was too quick and swung beneath the creature's claws. Rachel gasped and squeezed her eyes shut. She heard a grisly screech and a dying gurgle from the creature. Instinctively, she turned to go back the way she had come, but Aruj calmly placed his hands on her shoulders and held her gaze with his pearl eyes.

'The training rooms can be very frightening, Rachel, I do

understand. I took fright during my introduction. But there is a warrior in you, I sense it – and I know you can stomach the rest.'

It was more than he'd said to her the whole day, and she felt light-headed with the attention. She allowed them to show her each of the rooms further down the clay tunnel. They were all similar – swash-buckling beauties fighting and defeating icky creatures – until they reached three smaller rooms at the end of the passage.

'The Glamour Rooms,' Alinda said in explanation.

There were no weapons here, just faery creatures and … other faery creatures.

'The faeries' cunning is what makes them so dangerous,' said Aruj.

'In the wild,' Alinda continued, 'they have learned to bypass every form of attack. We can fight, and cast spells, but the faeries' wiles will always find a way around them.'

'All except glamour.'

'Their one weakness: An innate trust of their own kind. It is something they cannot unlearn. And with this, the Hunters found their strength.'

Rachel took it that one of each pair of faeries in each room was, in fact, a Hunter or a witch in disguise. A blue-skinned goblin paced one wall, its yellow eyes glowing in the shadow of its hunched frame. It kept a suspicious eye on the wispy, brown-skinned faery at the opposite side of the cell, who moved gracefully closer and closer. This watchful dance went on for some time until, finally, the goblin's shoulders relaxed in the gaze of the brown faery, and it allowed the other to approach. A flash of silver, and the dagger pierced the blue-skinned chest. Rachel cried out in horror, clamping her hands over her mouth.

'A faery's cunning,' Aruj's low voice repeated, 'is what makes them dangerous. They fawn and manipulate and win your pity; and that is how they make you weak. You must learn to look beyond the cunning to the cruelty; it is that, which will keep you safe.'

The blue-skinned goblin hadn't seemed cruel. And the tiny wood nymph Rachel had danced with earlier hadn't seemed cruel. But she trusted Aruj and his beautiful eyes, and decided she would never again be fooled by the play-acting of cute and cuddly faeries.

✳ ✳ ✳

'But the other three have already had a go. I'm just saying that I want to have a go as well!'

Una's black bob swayed from side to side as she looked between Jenny and Grace. Jenny stood firm, with her hands on her hips, looking down at the elfin-featured girl like a teacher instructing a toddler.

'And all I'm saying is that we'll wait and see what the Trial is first, and *then* decide. We'll pick the best person for the job.'

'But you'll never pick me. And I want a go!'

'A Cloaking Trial, Una,' Jenny was drifting dangerously into a patronising tone, 'if there's a Cloaking Trial, you'd be great at that.'

'And what if there is no Cloaking Trial? You can't stop me doing the next one. I'm on this team as well, you know.'

Grace sighed as she slid into her half-hammock. They'd been arguing like this since dinnertime. It was near lights-out, Rachel still wasn't back and everyone was on edge.

'Grace, can't I do the Trial tomorrow?'

'Of course you can do it if you want to.'

'No,' Jenny said forcefully. 'We pick the competitor after the Trial is announced, and play to our strengths. How else are we meant to win?'

'We're not here to win, Jenny, remember?'

'I am.'

'Yeah,' Una scoffed, 'not that you're insanely competitive or anything.'

'Look, I just want to show Meister and her snooty cows that they're not better than us. Because they're not. We're awesome. Look at what Rachel did today. And Adie and Delilah – well, I know we didn't win that one – but they showed off some serious skills–'

'And I'd just embarrass you.'

'No, it's not that …' Jenny's voice became low and serious as she changed tack. 'These Trials are dangerous, Una.

They can be deadly.'

'Deadly, schmeadly. I'm having a go.'

Grace raised her hand in the air.

'I vote Una does the Trial tomorrow.'

Adie nodded and raised her hand. Jenny's determined gaze fell on Delilah, but the small girl just said, 'I don't mind.'

'Yay,' Una said with a grin, and crawled into her alcove.

Defeated, Jenny dropped into the canal bed beside Grace.

'We're not here to win,' Grace whispered gently.

'It's not about winning the whole thing, it's about us and–'

Grace was surprised to hear Jenny's voice crack, then her friend shook her auburn hair and turned away.

✳ ✳ ✳

Grace awoke to a gentle prodding in the shoulder. The candelabras weren't lit yet, so it was still night.

'Hey,' Una whispered, prodding her again, 'you awake?'

Grace rubbed the sleep out of her eyes and stirred.

'Una? What's wrong?'

'Nothing. I can't sleep, it's too cold.'

'I've a couple of extra jumpers if you need them.'

'Nah, I've loads of clothes to lie on. The cold from the stone just gets through.'

'Oh, Una, would you not try the hammock again?'

Una shook her head but stayed sitting on the ledge.

'Grace. What if I'm rubbish?'

80

Grace rubbed her eyes again.

'What?'

'Tomorrow. What if I'm rubbish and I lose?'

'You won't be rubbish, Una.'

'What if I lose?'

'Then you lose. Who cares?'

'Jenny does.'

Grace pulled herself onto the ledge and put a hand on Una's arm.

'You'll be great tomorrow, no matter what happens. And don't worry about Jenny. I think she's going through … I don't know, something. She's not always as tough as she seems, you know?'

Una nodded.

'Okay. Thanks. And sorry for waking you.'

'Anytime.'

'Grace?'

'Yeah?'

'Wanna play I Spy?'

'Not really.'

''Kay. Night night.'

'Night.'

7

dragon Fodder

Exquisite; that was the only word Rachel could use to describe the banquet. Like Marie Antoinette, she sat at the head of the table, a row of golden candelabras perched amongst plates of glorious-looking food in front of her. Roasted chickens, drowning in juices, crunchy potatoes and honey-roasted carrots. In the centre of the table there was even an entire roasted suckling pig with an apple stuffed in its mouth. It grossed her out to look at it, but the two rows of glamorous Hunters on either side more than made up for it.

For dinner, they had all dressed to impress. The garb was still pirate-like, but the leather jerkins and loose blouses were draped in jewels and fine accessories. Some had close-cut or shaved hair, others long plaited styles like that of Alinda. She noticed a few other pearl-eyed diners, and presumed them to be more members of the Morgane tribe. Everyone appeared to be clear-skinned and glowing with health, and everyone looked wealthy and sophisticated – they were like a band of aristocratic adventurers, rich with unburied treasure. Rachel sighed in contentment, cutting elegantly into the small pieces of chicken on her gold-plated dish.

'This evening's banquet is in honour of Rachel of Dunbridge,' Aruj said, raising his glass and bowing at Rachel. 'To this year's victor of the Glamour Trial.'

There was a warm, but refined, cheer of congratulations, and the clinking of glasses, and Rachel blushed fiercely.

She spent the evening listening to stories of adventure and terror; the vanquishing of the most evil and brutal of creatures, and the heroism and bravery of the Hunters. They were hair-raising stories that scared her, but they also sparked a fire in her soul. This life of beauty and grandeur, but full of excitement and valour, was one she could never hope to experience. It was like something out of another time, when there were still new lands to explore and people were noble and full of courage. She wished she could stay longer than just an afternoon.

'It is late,' Alinda said to her towards the end of the meal. 'Perhaps you would like to stay the night? Your accommodation would be more than comfortable, I promise you.'

Rachel could have kissed her.

✷ ✷ ✷

'Origination!'

Grace's eyes remained fixed on Lady Hecate's figure perched high on the scaffolding opposite, but she could almost feel Una's face turn scarlet. The bleachers had resumed their position outside the barriers of the arena, making way for a number of wooden structures and tunnels randomly erected on the dry muck. On one end, to Grace's left, there was a break in the barrier that left a pathway out of the stadium, through the bleachers and the castle.

'The primary competitor,' Lady Hecate's voice echoed, 'will originate a creature to do battle in the outdoor enclosure.' She waved her hand indicating the pathway through the barrier. 'The remaining competitors of each team will survive within the battle area, and may protect themselves only with basic charms. Use of more complicated magic for protection or attack will result in immediate *disqualification*. This is a battle like no other, and you *will* respect the rules.' She eyed the Dunbridge team pointedly. 'Originated companions will fight to the death, victory going to the team with the surviving companion. Your creatures may attack witches of opposing teams, though not the primary competitor. All teams will now take their places, with primary competitors along the barrier.'

'No way,' Jenny whispered urgently to Grace, 'it's far too

dangerous. Una can't handle this. Rach still isn't back, so we're one down–'

'Then Rach is safer than we are,' Grace interrupted.

'Yeah, I guess. But I don't know what these basic charms are, do you? We'll be defenceless against any other companions. You or I should be doing the origination. It's for Una's own good.'

'Una would be safest as the primary competitor.' They both looked surprised at the tiny girl that suddenly stood between them. Delilah had been in her quiet funk for so long, it was strange to hear her voice. 'She can't be attacked by any other team. I can do a few basic charms to protect the rest of us. All we have to do is hold out until the game is over.'

'Then that's the plan,' Grace said firmly.

Grace, Jenny, Delilah and Adie were shuffled through the arena out into a huge pen that stretched to the farthest of the castle walls. It was enclosed by a short fence, only waist high, that was splintered and broken by the twisting roots and branches of a soot-coloured ivy that grew over it and through it. The black ivy sported flame-coloured leaves, and stretched three stories high, forming a massive dome over the enclosure. It kept out much of the daylight, and made Grace feel like they were underground.

Her heart went out to Una, who stood at the edge of the enclosure, taking deep breaths with an expression that was somewhere between scared and shocked. Grace smiled at her and Una suddenly brightened with fake enthusiasm, giving a double thumbs-up.

'Witches and witches,' Madame Three's voice squawked throughout the enclosure, 'ready your souls and your magic fingers. Begin origination. One, two, and three and … begin!'

There was an uncertain start to this muddled instruction, but Hawk Falls were quick as ever. The purple-haired girl was their originator, and she conjured a silver-furred bear, large and fierce, with canines that dripped with black saliva. The Raven team wasn't far behind with a vicious-looking crow the size of a car, with red eyes and horrible talons. Grace's heart thumped in her chest as, all around her, terrifying animals leapt into existence. She thought of the mangled monkey-deer that Una had conjured during their first lesson in origination and despaired. But the creature curled at Una's feet was no mangled anything. Its scaly tail unfurled to reveal a pointed head and a long, graceful neck, covered in sharp barbs. It planted its reptile feet, letting out a piercing shriek, then lowered its towering gaze to its master below.

'*Una*!' Grace was filled with pride.

'Grace,' Una cried out as if her friend hadn't seen. 'Look at what I did!'

'I know, it's unbelievable!'

Una beamed as her friends cheered, until her dragon companion shuffled forward, leaning its face close to hers. Una's expression turned to horror.

'It's gonna EAT me.'

'What?' said Grace. 'No, Una, it just wants to know what to do. Just tell it what to do.'

Una scrambled away from her dragon that loyally followed as she sprinted towards the girls.

'Una!' Jenny cried. 'It's your companion. It'll do what you want, just concentrate.'

'It's gonna EAT me!'

'It can't eat you,' Grace yelled as Una barrelled through them. 'It is you.'

'It can eat us though, right?' Jenny said.

Grace glanced up at the scaly creature that had now taken flight, confused and agitated by its lack of instruction.

'Yep.'

'Fudge. *Run.*'

Racing through the dimness the girls tried in vain to turn Una back. She was leading the pack and, as long as she ran, the dragon followed. Grace's foot snagged on a root and she fell face-first into the mud. She rolled over, stunned, and her view was filled with the head of a giant praying mantis. Its mandibles worked like it was already chewing as it dove towards her face. But powerful jaws immediately clenched around the mantis's head and ripped it clean off.

Grace squealed as she was wrenched to her feet by Adie and Jenny. Una's dragon had saved her life, but the animal seemed as eager to bite her head off as it had the insect's head.

'Run,' Delilah said, swiftly clenching a fist to her mouth, kissing her fingers and splaying them at the dragon. Little bursts of silver stars swarmed the companion's head, making it sniff and snort and then sneeze.

'Run!' Delilah said again.

'That won't stop it for long.' Jenny's breathing was laboured. 'Can't you do something stronger?'

'Basic charms only,' Delilah reminded her. 'That's as strong as they get.'

'Great.'

Through the dappled daylight they hurried on. The noise of the place was immense with companions battling each other, huge bodies occasionally slamming to the ground as, one by one, the giant animals fell and evaporated into nothing.

'*C-caw, c-caw.*'

Grace was too slow to react, and the Ravens' giant crow swooped down, gripping Delilah in its savage claws and taking off. But the dragon already had eyes on the tiny girl that had made it sneeze. It crashed into the bird mid-air, and Delilah was dropped to the ground, struggling to remain conscious. Adie covered her as the two animals scrapped, showering those below with feathers and scales. Just ahead, beneath a low canopy of flame-coloured ivy, Grace spied the

Raven team, hiding.

'Those sneaky bloody Ravens,' Jenny snarled. 'Why did they go for Delilah?'

'She's good,' said Grace. 'And they know it.'

There was a final screech, and a feathered black body smacked to the ground, then popped into nothing. The dragon hovered above them, staring down, angry and per-plexed.

'Una!' Grace could see a bouncing black bob not far ahead as her friend ran back to them. 'Dismiss it.'

'No,' Jenny said.

'Dismiss it,' Grace shouted again as Una got closer.

'No.' Jenny gripped her arm and pointed to their right. 'It's all we've got.'

In the distance, the Hawk Falls girls stood together, una-fraid of attack now there were so few animals remaining. Victoria Meister mouthed instructions to her purple-haired team-mate, a cruel smile playing on her lips. Their bear's silver fur rippled in the faint light, its powerful muscles so apparent as it pounded towards them.

'She's going to kill us,' Grace gasped.

Now Una had re-joined the group on the ground the dragon paused, still frustrated, still without its master's com-mand.

'Take control of it, Una,' Jenny said, her eyes on the advanc-ing beast. 'Stop the Hawk Falls' bear.'

'Stop the bear!' Una shouted.

The dragon didn't move.

'Don't tell it what to do, *will* it. It's a part of you, it is you. Will it to do what you want.'

'I don't know *how*.' Tears streamed down Una's face.

'You do,' Grace said, 'just imagine it's you up there. You stop the bear. You save us. Please, Una.'

Una stared up, her face crumpling, but it was like she was trying to read a foreign language.

'I don't know how,' she sobbed.

'Please, Una,' Grace squeezed her shoulders. She could hear the huffing breath of the beast that was nearly upon them. 'Please, Una, *try*.'

But Una's shoulders sagged beneath her fingers. To use bigger magic was to risk disqualification; for Grace to originate a new beast was to condemn them all to the dungeons. But what choice did she have?

What happened next seemed to occur in slow motion. Mist billowed from the bear's nostrils. It was so close she could feel the thump of its feet through the ground. Her hands trembled as she pictured the creature she would soon bring to life but, in that instant, a sticky whiteness wrapped around her, snapping her and her friends together in a tight bundle, and leaving them hanging from the flame-leaved dome. Spindly legs crept over them, revealing the body of a gargantuan spider. They all shrieked in fright, but the arachnid slinked over them, shooting more sticky web at the growling bear beneath, until the silver-furred creature had rolled and grappled itself into a tacky ball of gossamer. Only when the beast was completely immobile, did the spider creep down and give a venomous bite through its own web. The bear writhed for a few seconds, before there was a popping sound, and the ball of web deflated.

'Everyone okay?'

'Gaukroger!' Adie squealed.

Boy-Adie tickled his spider under the chin and smiled up at the girls with his too-wide smile.

'That was close, huh?'

'I love you.' Una sounded utterly sincere.

Adie's nervous laughter was full of embarrassment.

'She just means … she means thank you. That was so nice. Una, your dragon.'

Una nodded sharply to dismiss her companion, leaving Gaukroger the winner of the Trial.

'Yeah, cheers for that Boy-Ad– … eh, Gaukroger,' Jenny said, trying to wriggle her way out of her web trap. 'That was very cool of you.'

'No problem,' Gaukroger replied. 'Anything for … well, you all seem okay, so that's … that's good. If you just hang on there, I'll get him to cut you down.'

Grace couldn't help feeling trepidation as the giant hairy body stood over them with skinny legs, biting at the sticky strands of white. The web pulled painfully at the hairs on her skin, and she had a sudden rush of inspiration. She whispered something in Jenny's ear, and the other girl smiled and nodded. As they were hoisted to the ground, both held on to as much gossamer as they could carry.

❊ ❊ ❊

'Stop the press!' Eder Verzerrt strode towards them, his eyes impossibly large behind his milk-bottle glasses. Peach trotted behind him, her smile as big as her lovely round face would allow. Eder grasped Una's hand and bowed until his forehead touched her fingers. 'The news story of the century: Dunbridge and their meteoric rise through the Trials.'

'Eh, we didn't win,' Una replied.

'Gaukroger won,' Adie said firmly.

'Tempest Bridge won,' Gaukroger gently corrected her. 'It was a team effort.'

'Indeed, indeed,' Eder quickly shook the tall boy's hand, 'and a splendid win it was too, you must be very proud. But you,' he spread his arms wide, enclosing the girls only, 'you are the story that everyone wants to hear. What a mottled group you make. A companion out of control, the rest of you running to keep up and *only one* using the permitted charms. Not to mention your missing member currently enjoying the hospitality of the Hunters' Mansion. I demand an immediate and candid profile from each— Beep-bee-beep, b-bee-beep, b-beeeep.'

'Eder would be very grateful,' Peach didn't miss a beat, 'if you would join him in the dining room for an informal chat. He'd love to know a little more about each of you.'

'And Gaukroger,' Adie said quickly. 'He did win the Trial today.'

'Of course,' Peach said, with warm politeness. 'I'd love to hear about the training at Tempest Bridge.'

'It's pretty standard,' Gaukroger blushed and was clearly aware he was being included for politeness' sake, 'but I'll tell you anything you want to know.'

Eder's twitching and beeping continued as the odd group made their way to dining hall. Jenny fell behind and whispered as Grace turned away from the others.

'I stashed the web stuff in one of the gondolas,' she said. 'Where are you going?'

'Just … to the library.'

'Again? What for?'

'Oh, you know me and books. Looove my books.'

Grace was rubbish at lying and scratched her face to hide any reddening of her cheeks. Jenny looked suspicious for a moment.

'Alright, but you'd wanna keep this visit short if you're going to grab dinner before the kitchen closes.'

'Mmm,' Grace said, rubbing her belly mockingly. 'Can't wait for more of that gorgeous stuff.'

Stop it, she thought to herself, *you're making it worse*.

This time Jenny stared at her for more than a moment.

'See you soon, then,' was all she said.

Grace nodded and hurried away. She would have to make it quick. She fingered the map in her pocket that she had torn out of the green-covered library book. She had felt a terrible pang of guilt about tearing out the page – her mum had taught her that defacing a book was a worse crime than stealing – but desperate times called for desperate measures. Trouble was, she didn't know what scale the map was drawn to, so she had no idea how far it would be to the edge of the island.

She was surprised when she found the main door of the castle unguarded, and even more surprised to find it unlocked. Clearly the students were free to come and go as they pleased, though apparently no-one did. She glanced around, making sure the coast was clear, before pulling open the heavy iron-studded door and slipping outside. As she blinked against the green hue, she could have sworn she heard footsteps behind her but, when she swung around, there was nobody there. Feeling nerves set in, she unfolded the map and headed out across the barrenness towards the woods.

8

THE FERRYMAN

Rachel blinked in the shaft of light that shone through the break in the silk curtains. It was morning, and none of it had been a dream. She turned over and smiled, taking in every inch of the yellow room that she had so desperately wanted to see the day before. The bedroom was like the five-star hotel rooms she had seen on tv. It wasn't just a bedroom. Beyond the four poster bed that was insanely comfortable, there was a chaise longue and two armchairs, then another section of the room that contained a small breakfast table and chairs, with vases of silver flowers, and draping silk everywhere.

She was conscious that, back at Tithon Castle, her friends were much less comfortable. They might also be worried about her, but she couldn't bring herself to get out of bed and end the fantasy until there was a gentle knock on the door. Alinda's smile was as glorious as morning as she placed a plate of fresh fruit on the table.

'Breakfast,' she said. 'And I brought some fresh clothes, if you would like to change.' Rachel's heart skipped a beat when she saw the leather corset, breeches and blouse draped over Alinda's arm. 'And there is a scouting party heading for the river today, if you would like to join us.'

'Oh, I'd love to,' Rachel stammered, not wanting to turn down the invitation, 'but my friends—'

'We can send a message to Tithon on your behalf. You have no need to be concerned.'

Rachel gazed at the soft cotton blouse and decided not to worry.

✷ ✷ ✷

The ground was rock, cracked and full of fissures, and Grace had to keep an eye on her feet. She stumbled often as she tried to decipher the map and walk at the same time, but she was sure she was heading in the right direction. The entrance to the woods was just short of the river, which curved through the barren rock, sweeping through the trees, and a few metres in she found what had once been a path. It was overgrown now – clearly no-one had been there for years – but the vegetation was shorter and sparser, and she could follow the trail without too much trouble. She fought off the feeling of eeriness, telling herself there was nothing to fear, but she couldn't ignore that there was something very strange about these woods. There wasn't a sound. Not a single sound. No birds singing, no wind whistling, no scurrying of little animals in the bushes. The woods were silent. There was the barest rustling of leaves by a gentle breeze, but that was all. Where were all the animals?

This isn't my world, she told herself firmly. *Maybe there are no little animals in Hy-Breasal.*

But she didn't believe it, because there were always animals in woodland, but also because of the nature of the silence. There was something expectant in it. Like the creatures were there, but they were holding their breath, watching and waiting.

She let out an involuntary shiver when she finally cleared the trees, and stepped out onto a pebble beach. She'd reached the edge of the island.

It stretched as far as she could see in either direction, but the thick fog that sat on the water obscured her vision. She had never seen mist so dense, and the closer she moved to the shore, with the spray of seawater dampening her skin, the more tired she felt. The trek through the woods must have been harder than she thought. She ambled down the beach, slipping on wet pebbles, and almost forgot why she gone there in the first place. Until she saw a light in the fog.

Beneath it the silhouette of a row boat became clearer and

darker until she could make out the hooded figure that stood on the bow. His grim fingers gripped the pole that held the lamp and he remained motionless until Grace was within speaking distance.

'Can you pay?' His voice was like sandpaper, rough, gritty, and monotone.

'I don't know,' Grace said, her own voice high and wobbly with fear.

'Can you pay?' he repeated.

'What's the price?'

Jenny's warning sounded in her head and Grace felt sure of hearing the words, *your soul*. But the Ferryman swung the lamp-pole and suddenly Grace was racing through Tithon castle in her mind. Rooms rushed into her mind's eye, some she recognised, most she didn't, until Madame Three appeared, her arms draped eagerly around what looked like a massive snow globe. Inside was a lifesize silver-plated statue and, at its feet, the most beautiful blue rose made of pure, glittering sapphire. The rose swam in Grace's vision and she was sure.

'I ... I don't think I can get that,' she said, her head still reeling.

'After the moon sets in the west, thrice,' was the answer.

'Three moonsets ... you mean, three days from now? You will take us home three days from now?'

Water lapped against the boat and the Ferryman swayed.

But he didn't speak again.

'If I can't get the rose. What if …? Can we pay with something else? What if we don't make it to the ferry three days from now? Will you wait?'

Nothing but the water lapping. Somehow the boat and its Ferryman drifted back into the fog, until even the light of the lamp had disappeared, and she was alone on the beach.

'When three moons have set.' The voice was nothing more than a breeze over the water.

Rachel plucked at the boned corset, trying not to let anyone else see, and cursed herself for eating so much lunch. Life at the Hunters' Mansion moved slowly, despite their action-filled existence, and the scouting party had not left until the afternoon. After dressing, she had stood in front of the mirror for a full ten minutes, taking in the wonderful sight of herself as an old-world privateer. She looked gorgeous, and she didn't care who knew it. The only drawback to the outfit was that the midday meal had been as lavish as dinner the night before, and she had tried a bit of everything. Now the corset, which had cinched in her waist beautifully, was digging into her ribs. The other corset-wearers looked lithe and stoic, and not at all uncomfortable.

You must just get used to it, she thought. *Or maybe your ribs squish in after a while.*

'Bogles off the port bow!'

She glanced to the left, and saw a clump of grey scatter in the wake of the boat. They hadn't yet reached the river and the boat, smaller than the ship Aruj had piloted, scraped speedily along the barren landscape.

'Ha ha!' A blonde Hunter raised her bow, firing an arrow into the fleeing creatures.

Rachel looked to Aruj, who lounged against the side of the boat next to her.

'Bogles are vicious,' he said, 'but of very little threat. Gallant is wasting arrows.'

Gallant overheard, and winked at them, before firing another overboard.

'What kind are you looking for?' Rachel asked.

'There are rumours,' Aruj replied, 'of Merrows moving upriver. Merpeople are rarely seen in freshwater, and their gathering here is suspicious.'

'Gathering, in general, has become our greatest concern.' Alinda stood on the other side of Rachel. With her eyes on the river she looked almost weary. 'Breeds do not mingle, but of late we have found more and more species together, in groups. Their numbers are increasing in this area and this *gathering* suggests a strategy of some kind.'

'You think they're going to attack you?'

'It is possible.'

'Merrow!'

The boat had reached the river, and this time the whole scouting party jumped into action. They fired arrows, but only into the water. Where each one landed a flare soared into the air, and hovered, like a satellite in the sky.

'You're not going to kill them?' Rachel felt relieved.

'This is a scouting party only,' Alinda reminded her. 'We will mark their positions along the river, and return when we are sure we have found—'

She was interrupted when the boat suddenly swung to the left side. Rachel was thrown to the floor and, as the boat tipped even further, she clung to the mast to keep from falling overboard.

'A merrow has hold of the stern!' a voice shouted.

She looked back, and the creature gripping the back of the boat turned her legs to jelly. It wasn't any mermaid she had seen in cartoons. It was easily three times the size of a man. It did have the scaly bottom half of a fish, but its upper body was not human. It had a torso, and arms, but a ridged fin ran the length of its spine, and its head was shaped like a moray eel. A protruding snout was filled with razor-sharp teeth, and it had a huge mane of fleshy tentacles that lashed around its terrible head. It held fast to the gunwale, shaking the boat with powerful arms, and smashing its tail against the keel.

The boat groaned against the pull; spraying river water dampened the mast, making it slippery. Rachel was losing her grip.

'Help,' she yelled, scrambling to keep hold.

Her arms ached as the stern dipped lower and lower into the river, finally taking on water. The wood was too slick and she slipped, sliding inexorably down into the horrible embrace of the merrow. His mouth full of barbed teeth was just inches away, and his breath was cold and putrid. She tried to scream but no sound came out. The merrow raised one webbed hand …

Chunk.

Rachel opened her eyes just as Aruj grasped her collar and swung her behind him. In his other hand she saw the flash of a sword, and there was a pained, gurgling cry. She closed her eyes again, and didn't dare open them until the sound had stopped. Aruj stood panting, his sword dripping with greyish liquid, his beautiful skin dark and shining in the sunlight.

Rachel slid and floundered, trying to get up, but her legs were useless. Without a word, Aruj picked her up and carried her to the bow, as if the deck were made of velcro and she weighed nothing.

He was so freaking cool.

Grace didn't feel confident about stealing the sapphire rose, but when she left the beach behind she felt a new surge of energy. She wasn't tired anymore, and was able to pick up the pace through the woods as daylight faded. Finally, there was noise in the trees, the *whishy whishy* sound of the wind through the leaves. And fireflies. In the darkness the woods were dotted with the white light of fireflies glowing in the bushes. In pairs. Like eyes. Grace looked over her shoulder and picked up the pace again.

As night fell the sound of the wind became more distinct, like whispers. And in that moment, Grace grew very afraid.

Wishy, wishy

Witchy, witchy

Naughty witch, bad witch

The fireflies seemed to blink in pairs, and she knew now that they weren't fireflies at all, but that this wood was full of little creatures watching her.

Naughty witch, bad witch

Witchy-witch

Kill *the witch*

'I'm not a witch!' she screamed, breaking into a run.

The whispering echoed through the trees and the eyes were everywhere, but she didn't slow down until she felt solid rock beneath her feet. Stumbling over the fissures in the stone, her heart pounded in her chest until she pushed through the huge iron-studded door and closed it behind her. Panting with relief, she went to find the nearest gondola, leaving the door as she had found it, unlocked.

✳ ✳ ✳

'Hey, where ya been?'

Una was clambering awkwardly into a boat on the canal, with Adie and Delilah beside her.

'Library,' Grace gasped, resisting the urge to hug her friends as she squashed in behind them.

'Well, you missed a trick. That Eder bloke's a laugh and a half.'

'We're getting a special write-up in *The Lyceum Gazette*,' said Delilah.

'Splendid.'

'And I don't think Gaukroger's even getting a mention,' said Adie, 'and he's the one who saved us all.'

'After I was the most rubbish person ever,' Una said. 'God bless him.'

'Don't be so hard on yourself, Una. That dragon was epic.'

'And nearly ate you all. I'm so sorry and I swear, from now on, I'll shut up and do as I'm told. I'm no good to anyone.'

'Hey,' Grace slapped her on the shoulder, 'that's my friend you're talking about.'

'And besides,' Adie said, smiling, 'we've got a surprise that's bound to cheer you up.'

She winked at Grace as the gondola took off at full speed.

✴ ✴ ✴

Jenny must have snuck off during the dinnertime interview to work on their surprise in the Venetian Room. As the gondola sailed to a stop, they all looked up at the sticky web that spanned the width of the room. It was close to a web-shape, though not as pretty as a spider would make, with a shallow sack of gossamer in the middle, suspended high above the floor. Jenny was still in the air, putting the finishing touches to the ladder on the wall.

'It was Grace's idea,' she said, smiling down at Una.

'What was?'

'Your new bed,' said Grace.

Una stared up in puzzlement.

'You climb up the ladder here,' Jenny said, dropping gently to the ground, 'then across into the bed bit in the middle.'

'That's Jenny's design, by the way,' said Grace. 'Pure genius.'

Una didn't say anything, but slowly climbed the ladder, crawled across the web and disappeared into the sack-bed. A contented sigh arose from its depths.

'Is it comfy?' Grace asked. 'And warm enough?'

Una's head appeared over the edge of the bed and nodded. Her eyes were full of tears.

'Thanks, you guys.'

'You're welcome. Sleep tight.'

9

SOUNDS IN THE NIGHT

Rachel lay curled on the silk covers of her yellow silk bed. She was exhausted, exhilarated – and embarrassed. It hadn't occurred to her on the ride back to the mansion – she'd still been too awestruck by Aruj's valiant rescue – but as she sat at dinner she realised she'd been absolutely useless on the boat. No-one else had slipped down the deck and nearly been eaten alive by a giant merman. As soon as she could, she had politely excused herself and gone to her room.

There was a gentle knock on the door and she heard Alinda's voice.

'May I come in?'

'Sure.' Rachel sat up quickly, smoothing her hair and straightening her corset.

Alinda sat gently on the edge of the bed and smiled.

'I hope you weren't hurt this afternoon.'

'No, not at all. Thanks to Aruj. And, em … I wanted to thank you for letting me go on the scouting party. And for everything. It's been amazing. But … I think I should go back to the castle.'

Alinda looked disappointed.

'Oh, we had hoped you would stay on a little longer.'

'I would, it's just … I don't know how the Trials are going, and I'm worried about my friends.'

Alinda's face brightened and Rachel was struck again by the beauty of her pale eyes and silver hair.

'Is that all? But they can visit.'

'Really?'

'Tomorrow, if you'd like.'

'Brilliant! That would be great, thanks so much.'

'So you'll stay?'

Rachel felt the humiliation of the scouting boat melting away. She nodded.

'I'm so glad,' the woman said. She reached out and tucked a stray strand of hair behind Rachel's ear. 'Because I believe you have a gift, Rachel. And with the right guidance your future will be a bright one.' She rose and did her glide-walk to the door. 'Sleep well.'

'Goodnight.'

Rachel changed into one of the light cotton nightdresses from her chest of drawers, and crawled under the covers.

But she was too excited to sleep. She was looking forward to seeing the girls the following day but, if she was honest, it was Alinda's words that had her mind racing. *With the right guidance*. Did she mean her guidance? Did she intend to invite Rachel to stay and train with the Hunters? They clearly valued glamour spells above all else, and Rachel had a knack for them. Was she destined to be a Hunter? Would she get to live the incredible life she had been envying since she arrived at the mansion? She turned her face into her pillow, not sure who she was hiding her smile from. It was hours before her eyes finally felt heavy.

Scraaatch.

Her tired eyes snapped open. She heard it again.

Scraaatch.

It was coming from her bedroom door.

'Alinda?'

Scraaatch.

Rachel sat up, listening for a voice. But there was none.

Another minute passed and she eased out of bed and crept over to the door, pressing her ear against the wood. In the silence, she whispered,

'Is someone there?'

SCRAAATCH.

She stumbled backwards into the dresser, snatching a pointed figurine from beside the mirror as she steadied her-self. Tiptoeing back to the door, she whispered again,

'Is someone there? I have a weapon.'

Steeling herself, she clasped the doorknob and opened the door a crack. She couldn't see anyone. Taking a deep breath, she wrenched the door open and jabbed the figurine into thin air. Nothing. The hall was dark and quiet.

Except for a little whimper.

It came from down the hall, to her right. It could have been a chair, scraped over a marble floor, but who would be moving about in the middle of the night? There. Again. It was fainter, further away, but this time it was longer and there was another sound behind it. A watery sound.

Rachel stepped out of her room, clenching the pointed figurine. She inched her way down the hall, her feet growing cold on the polished wood floor. She was almost to the gallery when her right foot slipped into something. She looked down to see a small puddle of water. Ahead of it she saw another, and another. They were like footprints, small footprints leading into the gallery and down the spiral staircase to the marble floor below. The marble felt like ice to her bare feet but, with its pale colour and the light of the moon creeping through the slatted windows beneath the curved ceiling, she could clearly make out the glint of the watery trail.

She had only seen this part of the mansion from the mezzanine and now, as she moved along the floor, she could see she was in a long room filled with ornate framed portraits on

109

the walls. But these portraits were different from the others in the mansion. They were much larger, and they were dark and grim. And all of them were of children.

In one, a blond boy, about three years old, held a toy in his hands. It was a wooden puzzle, painted bright colours, but his clothes were grey and black and his expression was full of woe. He was in a woodland setting, at night, and the branches of the trees were painted like creeping fingers, reaching out for him. In the dark leaves, fireflies glowed like eyes.

Another was of a pair of twins. One girl stood just outside the closed front door of a stone cottage, her palm flat against the wood, and a frightened, pleading look on her face. The second stood at the window, smiling from inside the house. Her eyes were smaller, and her chin and ears ever so slightly pointed. She looked self-satisfied, and appeared ignorant of the other girl's beseeching expression.

'Creepy,' Rachel whispered to herself.

As she neared the end of the gallery, there was another whimper, this time very close. She tightened her grip on the figurine, and slid into the shadows of the pillars lining the walls. Peeking around the gold mouldings, her eyes followed the small footsteps to the far corner. There, in a shaft of moonlight, a little boy sat curled against the wall.

He was no more than six or seven years old, and he was soaking wet. He shivered in a light, woollen nightgown, his black hair was streaked across his forehead and his huge green eyes were almost too big for his face. He was so cold his lips were turning purple. Rachel was sure he couldn't see her hidden in the shadows behind a marble pillar, but his huge eyes were fixed on her.

'Don't let them get me,' he whispered.

'I don't–' Her voice caught in her throat.

'Don't follow the light. Don't let them get me.'

She knew she should go to him – a little boy, cold and afraid – but she couldn't. Something wasn't right.

'Ssssssss!' The boy was sucking in a breath, reaching out his hands to her.

Suddenly he was on his feet, running towards her, hands outstretched, then whump!

He vanished. Dropped through the floor like he had just fallen off a cliff.

Rachel stood shaking. A puddle of water swelled where the boy had disappeared.

'Don't let them get me.'

The whisper echoed through the walls of the gallery, reverberating through the disquieting paintings of the children that all seemed to have turned their eyes to her. Then the sound faded to nothing, the children's eyes averted, and she was left alone in the cold and the moonlight.

✳ ✳ ✳

Unable to quench her own team spirit, Grace watched

Jenny gliding above her and silently urged her friend higher. They wouldn't win the Trials but, with displays like Jenny's today, they were putting on a good show. Hawk Falls sat on their right in the bleachers, making Jenny see red; Tempest Bridge, including Gaukroger, sat on their left, making Adie's cheeks red. Jenny was the obvious choice for this Trial anyway but, when Victoria Meister stepped forward to once again compete for her team, the fight was on.

There were four layers of shining crystals, each level a different colour, with green the highest. The players had to collect one of each colour. The snag was that the number of crystals dwindled the higher the level. Five players had already missed snatching white ones from the bottom layer, and lost immediately. Not Jenny though. She had soared up there, the third to snatch a crystal and deposit it in a basket on the ground.

'Your friend is doing great.' Grace turned to a tap on the shoulder, and saw a familiar sweet smile.

'Hey, Aura!' She glanced at the players again. 'You're ahead of us, though. Isn't that your team captain?'

The boy with long hair tied back was the second to grab a white crystal.

'Yep, that's Arick. He's excellent at flying. We're hoping to get a first on this one, we've only got a second and third so far.'

A boy beside Aura, who didn't look much older than her,

elbowed her in the side. 'No fraternising with the enemy!'

'Oh, we're not going to win the Trials, don't worry,' Grace told him cheerfully. 'Too many penalties. We're mainly just here to cause trouble.'

Aura giggled loudly and her team-mate scowled.

At a sudden *Oooooh* from the crowd, Grace turned back to find that the competitors were already up to the second-highest level. There was scrabbling for the crystals, the worst of it between Victoria and Arick. They both had a good grip on the large, blue crystal, and neither was willing to let go. They spun like a boomerang, faster and faster, until Victoria swung a knee into Arick's ribs.

'Oh no!' said Aura.

The boy still clung fast to the crystal until two more vicious kicks from Victoria, one to the arm and one to the head, sent him spiralling to the ground. He slowed his descent a little, but it wasn't enough, and he hit the ground with a crunch.

'Arick!' Aura leapt to her feet and ran to the arena, but the invisible barrier kept her out. 'Arick! Someone help him.'

Grace raced to her side, watching the crumpled figure on the ground.

'He's moving,' she said. 'I think he's okay.'

'Broken leg!' Madame Three's tremulous voice called without feeling. 'Balefire Warren, you may remove your competitor from the arena. The healer will chop off his leg, or arm, or any other bit necessary … perhaps his whiskers.'

113

Aura could step through the barrier then, closely followed by the rest of her team. Grace winced as they helped the tall boy to his feet and half-carried, half-dragged him into the castle.

'Is there any way we can tell Jenny to let go if Victoria grabs a green crystal first?' Adie said as Grace returned to her seat.

'You know she won't, no matter what we say.'

The four girls sat in silence, anxiously watching as the remaining competitors rose to dizzying heights, and the final level. Out of the corner of her eye, Grace saw Gaukroger take Adie's hand.

Grace's heart leapt and fell in one moment, as Jenny grabbed one of the three green crystals before Victoria caught her around the waist. They thrashed and twisted, quickly losing altitude, and Grace felt Una squeeze her arm before Jenny skilfully spun out of Victoria's grip and sailed to a rough, but safe, landing.

'Yes!' The girls leapt to their feet, cheering boisterously, and giddy with relief.

'We won,' Una shouted in Grace's ear. 'We won another one.'

But their victory was short-lived. Grace didn't see the stream of crackling energy that shot from Victoria's fingers, but she saw it ricochet off the crystal, still clutched in Jenny's hands, and fire straight into the struts that held the scaffolding and the three Supremes. The platform collapsed in a creaking cacophony of snaps and screams, and all three Heads of the Lyceum toppled into the arena, showered in woody debris. The dust settled and there was absolute silence.

Madame Three undulated from beneath the wreckage like a caterpillar. Her blonde curls were dishevelled and spiked with bits of timber.

'Dunbridge renegade,' she screeched, one finger pointed furiously in Jenny's direction. 'Death to all!'

'No,' Jenny cried. 'That wasn't me, that was–'

'SILENCE!'

Lady Hecate had pulled herself from beneath the remains of the platform, cracking her back and neck as she finally stood upright, her reddening face a clear indication of her mood.

'St John's of Dunbridge are denied this victory.'

'But Jenny didn't do anything–' Una cried before a chilling glance from Lady Hecate silenced her.

'This insolent child,' the woman snarled at Jenny, 'will be bound for her ineptitude.'

There was a gasp from the crowd, then a distant chime from inside the castle. The chiming got closer and closer until it became the unmistakable clanging of metal off stone. Something flew through the arena entrance, bouncing off bleachers and finally snapping around Jenny's ankle.

'*Ow!*'

'*That*,' the woman snarled again, 'will impose some much-needed control.'

Jenny looked up at her friends, apparently not in pain from the metal ring now closed around her ankle, and shrugged her shoulders. Behind her it took four students to help Lord Machlau to his feet. When all Supremes were standing, they walked grandly from the arena, leaving Grace and her friends perplexed as to what punishment Jenny had just suffered.

10

a whole new world

'This is well fancy.'

Rachel paused at the door and smiled at the sound of Una's voice. She checked her hair and blouse one more time, making sure the girls' first impression of her new look would be perfect. Her friends had been shown into one of the reception rooms off the main entrance hall. She had hoped they might be given a quick tour of the building, so they could soak in the opulence before she appeared, fashionably late and effortlessly casual. But Alinda had fetched her as soon as they had arrived. Still, the mansion was impressive enough even without a tour – they'd still be bowled over.

'Hello, everyone.'

She wasn't disappointed with their reaction. Grace's eyebrows nearly disappeared into her hairline, Adie and Delilah stood with open mouths and Jenny, who sat bent over in a chair, fiddling with something on her ankle, looked up and stared.

'Wowza,' Una said, clumsily replacing the gold-plated ornament she had plucked from the mantelpiece. 'You've been Swanned!'

'Well,' Rachel said, faking modesty as she swept a hand over her plaited locks, 'don't know about that, but they lent me some new clothes. Didn't have any clean ones with me.'

'Well then, A-plus to the Hunters for their clean clothes.'

'You do look gorgeous,' said Grace. 'But isn't that a little tight?'

She gestured to the corset that was, again, digging into Rachel's ribcage. She wasn't sure why it was still uncomfortable, she had eaten as little as possible at breakfast that morning. Jenny got to her feet and took a long look at her outfit.

'Where does your liver go?'

'Huh?' said Rachel.

'In the biology lab at school remember that half-a-body made of plastic? With all the internal organs that look kind of real? And the liver is humungous. It goes right there,' she pointed just below Rachel's ribs, 'so if you do that to your waist, where does your liver go?' She stared at the corset like she was working out a puzzle. 'All your intestines must be pushing it upwards.'

'Maybe it goes up into your throat,' said Una, leaning in to look into Rachel's mouth. 'Say aaaahh.'

'I'm loosening the laces, Rach,' said Grace.

'Don't!' Rachel exclaimed, 'I'm fine, I swear. It's comfortable, it's how they all wear them.'

'You're about to pass out, it's way too tight. Here.'

Rachel tried to keep Grace from grabbing the laces at the back of the corset, but gave up quickly. It was such a relief when the bones stopped digging into her sides and she didn't want to admit it, but she'd been feeling a bit light-headed.

'Much better,' said Grace, retying the laces with a little room to spare.

Rachel frowned looking down at herself; it wasn't a Barbie-doll waist anymore.

I can tighten it up when the girls leave, she thought to herself. Though being able to breathe was kind of nice.

'So,' said Una, tipping back into the seat of a chair, leaving her legs draped over the arm, 'how's it been in the posh house?'

Rachel grinned.

'*Amazing*. You wouldn't believe how gorgeous the rest of the mansion is. And they have banquets every night. And yesterday I went out with a scouting party and–'

'That's great,' Grace interrupted, 'but I've got some big news. I didn't want to tell you guys until I'd checked it out, but I know how we can get back home.'

'How?' asked Jenny.

'The Ferryman.'

'Oh, come one, we've talked about this—'

'It's easy to get to the boat and we don't have to sell our souls to get across. The ferry leaves in two days and we just need …' Grace paused, looking a little less sure, 'this sapphire rose thing. It's in the castle.'

'Where in the castle?' said Adie.

'In this big snow globe, in Madame Three's room.'

'How will we get that?'

'We'll find a way.'

'When in two days?' said Una. 'Morning? Evening?'

'I don't know, he didn't give a time. Morning, I guess. He's kind of … he's a bit mysterious, the way he talks.'

'Did you go and see him?' Adie looked horrified at Grace having left the castle grounds alone.

'Yes, and he was exactly where the book said he would be. So you see? It's definitely the boat home.'

She looked to Jenny who had one eyebrow raised.

'Definitely?' said Jenny.

'Yes!' A flush was rising in Grace's cheeks, and Rachel knew she was afraid of losing the argument. 'It's all straightforward. We pay him, we get on the ferry, we go home.'

'So straightforward that he *mysteriously* didn't give you an actual time of departure? Not exactly catching the boat to France at Rosslare, is it?'

'He said when three moons have set. That's two days from

now … in the morning, probably. It's … well, we're on a bloody magical island, it was never gonna be Rosslare!'

There was silence for a few moments, but Una, Adie and Delilah all looked hopeful.

'I still don't like the sound of him.' Jenny had parked herself back in the armchair with folded arms. 'I think we should find another way out.'

'Like some epic transportation spell?' Grace asked. 'And are you going to do it with that thing around your ankle?'

Jenny scowled and crossed her arms tighter.

'What is that thing?' said Rachel.

'A binding ring,' Delilah said quietly. 'It prevents her from doing any magic.'

'Really?'

Jenny stood up and lifted her arms out to the sides while her feet stayed fixed to the ground.

'Wanna see me fly? This is it. This is me flying.'

'I don't get it.'

'I can say all the verses I want, and build up the buzz, and mix up a potion, but I've got no juice.'

'She's juiceless,' said Una.

'Victoria Meister is really out to get us,' said Grace, 'and she got the Supremes to bind Jenny's powers. We're pretty sure we're out of the Trials too – thought we're not going to cry over that – but we've no idea what else she has in store. We need to get out of here. Now.'

Rachel plucked nervously at the sleeve of her blouse. This was too quick, she needed to think. Just last night she was sure she'd be offered the chance to stay and train with the Hunters. Now Grace was telling her they had to leave it all behind, immediately. She had intended to tell the others about the ghost in the gallery – she had been afraid to mention it to Alinda – but now she didn't want to add fuel to the fire. The girls would just see it as something else dangerous, another reason to leave.

'Alright,' Grace said firmly, 'who votes to break into Madame Three's room, steal the sapphire rose, and take the ferry home?'

Rachel's pulse quickened as, one by one, the hands went in the air. The blood was pounding in her ears before she realised everyone was looking at her.

'Rach?'

'Wait, Grace,' she stammered. 'If we … are you sure we should leave? Now, I mean?'

'What?'

'It's just that, this is a whole new world. One just for witches. How do you know we don't belong here?'

'What are you talking about?' Adie looked at her like she was a stranger.

'I mean that … what if this is where we're meant to be. Maybe this is our destiny. Maybe we could have wonderful lives here.'

'Wonderful lives?' Grace snapped. 'We've been here for four days and so far Adie and Delilah have nearly drowned, we've been attacked by a giant praying mantis and a silver bear, and Jenny's been electronically tagged.' Jenny stuck her foot in the air for emphasis. 'What are you thinking?'

Rachel couldn't tell them what she was thinking, they wouldn't understand.

'Never mind. But would it be okay for me to stay here until the ferry leaves? I could meet you on the beach, in the morning, day after tomorrow.' She went on quickly as the colour rose in Grace's cheeks. 'I mean, wouldn't it look suspicious if I insisted on going back to the castle with you, right after I promised I would stay a little longer? It might scupper your plans if they decide to keep a closer eye on you.'

Suspicious looks went all around the room. Rachel avoided them.

'Don't you miss home?' said Adie.

Rachel's eyes welled up at the thought of her parents, and she couldn't stop the tears.

'I don't mind if you want to stay here tonight and tomorrow,' Grace said suddenly, touching her arm. 'But how will you know where to meet us? I can describe it, but that's not very foolproof.'

'Oh, there are maps all over the place here, just point out where the beach is. Look! There's one right there, on the wall.'

123

She trotted over to the framed map and traced her finger along the coast.

'Here? Is it this beach here? Easy!' She kept babbling, nervous. 'Alinda will know where it is, anyway, if you're worried about me getting lost. The Hunters move through the woods all the time. They're really–'

Grace's soft look became suspicious again.

'You won't tell her what we're doing?'

'Of course not.'

The conversation became stilted after that and Rachel felt guilty that the girls weren't asked to stay for dinner. But even if it had been up to her, she wouldn't have invited them. They were killing the buzz that the Hunters' Mansion gave her, and she wanted to feel it for as long as she could. Before she was ripped from a life of adventure, and ferried back home.

* * *

Aura was waiting for the girls when they returned to Tithon. She stood just inside the castle walls as they shuffled messily down the steep gang-plank of the Hunters' ship. She was wringing her hands and her sweet smile was nowhere to be seen.

'Aura,' said Grace, 'what's wrong?'

'You have to come to the arena. The Supremes have summoned you.'

'Oh, God,' Jenny groaned, 'what did we do now?'

'It's my fault,' Aura said. 'I was telling Arick at breakfast how you all were invited to the Hunters' Mansion and Victoria Meister heard me. She … I don't know what she's done.'

'So little Miss Prissy's at it again. That's not your fault, Aura, don't worry.'

'Please hurry. They're all waiting.'

With a growing sense of doom, Grace and the others followed Aura to the stadium, where everyone sat in the bleachers excepting the Supremes and Hawk Falls, who stood in the centre of the arena.

'St John's of Dunbridge,' Lady Hecate declared in shrill tones, 'you have been accused of a grotesque crime, and must hereby stand before your accusers.'

Grace shivered beneath the gaze of the crowd, and apprehension filled her.

'Whatever that Victoria trollop is saying is rubbish,' said Jenny boldly to the Supremes. 'She's a jealous, stuck-up pain in my bum.'

'Trollop?' Una whispered.

'Got that from Mrs Quinlan,' Jenny whispered back.

'Nice one.'

Grace shook her head. She was frightened. This was something big, she could feel it, and she didn't think her friends had any idea.

'Ms Meister?' said Lady Hecate.

THE WATCHING WOOD

Victoria stepped forward, the head of a grey sable hanging from her throat, and extended an arm to point theatrically at Grace.

'I saw Grace Brennan with the Ferryman.'

You could have heard a pin drop and the Supremes' faces were like thunder. Grace, shocked, held her breath as she waited for more. But the smirk on Victoria's face told her that what she'd said was enough.

'What just happened?' Una whispered.

'I don't know,' Grace replied.

Was it that she had left the castle without permission? Was that enough to shock an entire stadium into silence?

'She's not a *witch*.' The gasped sentence came from somebody in the crowd and broke the quiet. Murmuring spread from the front row back, until there was a cacophony of excited chatter ringing in Grace's ears. She didn't know what to do until Jenny did the obvious.

'She's lying!' she shouted. The chatter stopped. 'Grace never left our sight. Whatever Ms *Meister* says, she's lying.'

The Hawk Falls purple-haired girl stepped forward and pointed.

'I saw Grace Brennan with the Ferryman.'

Then Victoria's bubble-running partner stepped up.

'I saw Grace Brennan with the Ferryman.'

All six girls pointed and accused. Grace's breathing was shallow and fast. She remembered the books from the rotten corner of the library. *Wickedness and the Human Fallacy. Homo Sapiens: The Wiccan Neanderthal.* And she could see now the look of utter disgust on the faces of the Supremes.

'This is very bad,' she whispered. 'Not being a witch here? I think it might be very bad.'

'Of course she's a witch,' Jenny jumped in with both feet once again. 'We're here to compete in the *Witch* Trials. We're all witches.'

'Witches who need the Ferryman to cross the water,' Victoria sneered.

'Yeah, well,' Jenny said, lifting her leg to remind them of the binding ring, 'some of us are currently challenged in that respect. So … you know … thanks for that.'

'Why cross the water at all?' Victoria looked too sure of herself. 'She's not a witch.'

'Do I have to come over there and shut you up?'

'She's not a witch.'

Jenny nudged Grace in the ribs and growled through gritted teeth.

'Say something. Say you're a witch.'

Grace was so dizzy with worry she thought she might faint. She felt another nudge.

'I am a witch!' The sound was high-pitched and strained coming from her tightening throat. 'I *am* a witch. I am a witch.'

'*I'm not a witch!*'

She jumped at the sound of her own frightened voice coming back at her. It was emanating from a ball in Victoria's outstretched hand.

'*I'm not a witch! I'm not a witch! I'm not a witch!*'

So there *had* been footsteps behind Grace when she left the castle that afternoon. Cloaked, Victoria must have followed her to the pebble beach, and recorded her terrified denials in the firefly woods.

'Backward beings,' Madame Three shrieked. 'Stealing our preciousness. They taint our very lives with their dirty beingness! To the dungeons!'

There was a cheer from the crowd. In the front row Grace could see Aura's troubled looks, her team stood and clapped, but she remained seated.

'Perhaps,' Lady Hecate said, quietening the noise. 'But by Wiccan Law we must follow the proper proceedings. An impartial court will decide their fate based on the evidence.' Her eyes turned on Grace. 'Until then, no more repellent forgery will be permitted in Tithon.'

Clanging in the castle.

'Oh, fudgeballs,' groaned Una.

Four binding rings clashed and banged their way to the arena, their metals ringing with vibration. Bruising pain hit Grace as one snapped around her ankle. Adie, Delilah and Una all cried out.

'To the Black Turret then?' Madame Three looked

eagerly at Lady Hecate.

'Lord Machlau?' she said.

The stooped Lord fired one finger in the air, pointing to a dark turret that stood at the far end of the castle, and Madame Three laughed in triumph.

'And then the dungeons,' she squealed. 'To squirm with the wrigglies and the ones that are squished.'

Lady Hecate paused.

'Quite.'

✳ ✳ ✳

Before she became queen, Elizabeth I had been locked in the Tower of London by her half-sister, Mary, who was afraid she'd try and nick the throne. Grace had seen a documentary once that showed some of the cells in the Tower, so she knew what to expect: small stone rooms, with archways that led nowhere, little daylight, damp-stained floors and ceilings, black and dark green mould up the walls. The Black Turret had all this and more – for in their cell, there was hardly any space to sit down, due to piles of old junk stacked against every available inch of wall.

The long walk up the seemingly endless spiral staircase had left Grace short of breath. She had considered their chances, if she and her friends were to make a break for it and try to run, but they were now without any magic, and surrounded by those with it. Madame Three had herded them into the turret like sheep, poking them with a sharp staff when they moved too slowly.

'Up the steps, one step, two step, one step … no talking with your loud legs. Move, move, move.'

The stout woman's weirdly plump face was the last thing they saw before the heavy door swung shut and there was the *clunk-clunk* of a key turning in the lock.

Una collapsed against the rusted remains of a bed frame that stood on end by one of the small windows.

'What the hell do we do now?'

'I'm sorry everyone,' Grace said, 'I'd no idea it would get us into this kind of trouble.'

'Grace,' Jenny said firmly, 'this isn't your fault. We'd have been set up by that Meister cow one way or another. We just have to find a way out of this.'

'How?'

'Delilah, you know more about this stuff than any of us. Is there any way to get the binding rings off?'

Delilah was sitting on her hunkers in the corner, her fingers hooked around the bars of a small cage as she peered inside.

'No,' she said softly, still distracted, 'not without magic.'

'Fudge!' Jenny's sudden shout made everyone jump. 'Sorry, sorry, lost it there for a sec. Sorry about that. Well then, we'll have to do a jailbreak the old-fashioned way.'

'Meaning?' Adie said.

'Climb out the windows and abseil down the turret.'

'You got some rope for that, Rapunzel?' Una said, leaning out one of the glassless windows. ''Cos it's a long way down.'

'Rope! That's what we need! There's bound to be something in all this rubbish. Come on.'

Half an hour, and a lot of digging later, Grace, Adie, Jenny and Una sprawled in various levels of discomfort, more depressed than ever. There was no rope. And nothing they could use as a substitute.

'Where do we pee?' Una said suddenly.

Grace looked around, but Jenny answered first.

'There's a bucket in that archway over there.'

'Ah, here! No way, that's totally inhumane.' She looked to the others as if one of them could materialise a bathroom, then crossed her legs. 'I'll hold it.'

Quiet fell as the room filled with the green-laced orange light of sunset. Grace looked to the corner and realised Delilah hadn't left her spot by the little cage.

The small girl felt her gaze on her and smiled. 'It's the wood nymph.'

'Huh?'

'From the Glamour Trial.' Delilah's fingertips gently traced the thin bars.

'Hey,' Jenny said, leaning in to get a good look. 'It *is* the nymph. They must stash him up here when they're not using him.' She poked a finger through the bars, then leapt back

131

and squealed. 'Ow! Bit me, little brat.'

'So cruel,' Delilah's voice was still soft. 'To use him. Treat him like a thing. And he's never free.'

Grace saw a single tear spill down Delilah's cheek as her fingers felt for the lock.

'Wait, Delilah!' said Grace.

But the small girl had already opened the cage door and sat back against the wall. The nymph remained crouched inside the bars; he'd been teased like this many times before. Delilah stayed clear of the cage and closed her eyes.

'He'll come out when he's ready.'

11

a witch trial

It lurked at the back of the cell, its breathing guttural and thick. She had caught a glimpse of it when she moved from the door to the far corner, but night was falling and, with no lamp inside the room, it remained disguised in the shadows. Except for its eyes. Two narrow flecks of grey, glowing in the darkness. They never blinked.

Arboraceous. That was how Aruj had described it. Black, branch-like limbs, sharp and angular, sick with rot. A triangular head, dead grey eyes, and a thin mouth full of needle-pointed teeth. Its woody claws scraped on the hard, clay floor as it moved.

Rachel couldn't glamour this breed, not without getting a closer look at it, and she hadn't reached the arboraceous section of the *Faery Encyclopaedia* she had been given to learn.

There were countless species of faery, she was sure she could never learn them all.

Aruj had advised against glamouring into the same species as you were trying to fool. It was safer to choose another species.

'It's too close to home,' he had said. 'A faery will usually recognise its own breed. And will easily reject that which is not.'

But Rachel reminded Aruj that she had glamoured a wood nymph to fool a wood nymph, and it had worked perfectly.

This time she picked a bogle. About two feet high, and grey in colour, she thought it somewhat resembled the creature that was making the hairs stand up on the back of her neck, though it was smaller and much less threatening. To choose a more commanding faery, she felt, would be the wrong way to go with this one. He was the scarier animal in the room, and she meant to keep it that way.

It was slow work. As a bogle, she pottered about the floor, throwing the dark thing playful glances, then ignoring it and pretending she had found something terribly amusing on the dusty floor. Then she'd jump up and smile at it again.

I'm harmless, was the message she was trying to give out. *You can come as close as you want.*

The glamour covered her Hunter clothes and, beneath her leather jerkin, the silver dagger.

After some time the creature began to move a little closer.

It wasn't so much interested in her as it was less bothered by her presence. Its pacing became more relaxed and took up more of the cell. The nearer it came, the more Rachel could hear of its breathing, the *glig glig glig* of exhaled air through its mucus-coated throat. She tried to stay calm, forcing herself to turn her back occasionally, so that her pottering looked innocent.

'B*ooo*gle.'

The voice was so inhuman, she didn't immediately recognise it as speech. The word sounded like something produced by one of those talking dogs or cats on the internet, a mouth forming sounds it wasn't designed to make.

'B*ooo*gle.'

She had her back to the creature for the last phlegmy syllable and when she turned around the grey eyes were right in front of her. She jumped, the eyes faltering as her glamour wavered.

Concentrate, she said to herself. *And ignore the* …

Teeth. Like yellow needles. More than she could count. The gremlin head dipped from side to side, taking a careful look at her. Something ticked in its mouth, like it was tutting. She swallowed hard, trying not to stare into the dead eyes. Up close its scent was pungent – the smell of dank forest, blighted by fungus and mould. It stung her nostrils and made her want to sneeze. As it breathed on her, the smell was infinitely worse.

'B*ooo*gle.'

She trembled, trying to block out the voice and the smell and … With the sound of snapping twigs the creature shot away from her and clung to the wall, its long, splintered limbs throwing eerily sharp shadows.

'*Hesssssss.*' The hissing was so loud she could feel it rattling her inner ear.

She had felt the glamour fall, just for a split second, but it was long enough for the creature to see something. She dropped the façade altogether, and pulled the dagger from beneath her jerkin. But the creature had braced itself against the clay wall, inches from the door, ready to pounce. She couldn't get past it.

'*Hesssssss.*' Its black tongue wriggled through its teeth.

'Aruj?' Rachel whimpered.

There was no sound from outside.

'Aruj? Help me. Please!'

Still nothing.

'*Hesssssss!*'

The creature bared its awful yellow teeth and crouched into its creaking limbs.

'*Aruj!*'

It sprang at her, like some giant insect, pinning her to the ground, its pointed claws and knees digging into her legs and arms. She screamed and wrenched herself to one side, but the creature rolled her until it pinned her again. With the stench of it clouding the air, the wicked mouth pulled wide and lunged at her face.

'*Hesssssss*!'

The dagger pierced the animal just under the ribs. Sticky brown sap spilled over Rachel's hand as she turned her head away from it and cried into the clay, waiting for the hissing to stop.

Finally, the wheeze faded to nothing and the whole weight of the jagged body sagged on top of her. With her eyes still closed Rachel lay frozen beneath the creature and her tears turned the clay to mud.

'Enter the accused!'

The girls looked around, perplexed. They had been brought to a makeshift courtroom, and sat on the right behind a table facing a high bench and three empty chairs. To their left sat the Hawk Falls girls, perfectly prim and facing the bench with barely concealed smirks. Those students that had been quick to queue that morning had succeeded in filling the limited seating in the pews behind them. There was no seating for a jury, so Grace had to assume this would be judge-only trial.

'Enter the accused!' Madame Three yelled again. She stood next to the bench like a bailiff.

'We're already here,' Una said.

Madame Three squinted at them, even though she had already poked Grace twice with her staff before the proceedings had begun.

'Enter the judges!' she yelled, apparently satisfied.

Lord Machlau shuffled in to take the empty seat far right of the bench. Lady Hecate followed him grandly. When both were seated, Madame Three stamped her way behind the bench and sat down. Grace gaped.

'*They're* the judges?' Adie whispered.

'Oh, what?' Jenny said out loud. 'That's just mental.'

'Silence in the courtroom.' Lady Hecate banged a gavel on the bench. 'St John's of Dunbridge, you are accused of being human, and of using Wiccan powers to bring disgrace to the Witch Trials of Tithon Castle. How do you plead?'

'Guilty,' a voice yelled at the back.

'Shut up!' Jenny yelled back. 'Innocent! We're innocent.'

'Very well,' said Lady Hecate. 'In that case your accusers will present all evidence against you, and you shall rebut with any evidence in your favour.'

'Fat chance,' said Madame Three.

Lady Hecate held up a hand.

'Both sides shall be heard before the defendants are declared guilty.' She caught herself. 'Or innocent … in the unlikely event that they *are* innocent.'

Madame Three snorted. Jenny looked at Grace.

'Going well so far, don't you think?'

✷ ✷ ✷

'And then I slipped, just inside the dining hall. It was a very painful fall, and when I looked–'

'Was it gooey?' Madame Three asked, peering at the witness over a pair of thin-rimmed spectacles that she had donned in order to take notes during the trial.

'I'm sorry?'

'The substance on which you slipped, was it gooey?'

'I …' the girl hesitated, apparently trying to judge the look on the Supreme's face. 'Yes, yes, it was gooey.'

'Mm-hmm, human goo,' Madame Three nodded knowingly, then returned to scribbling her notes.

'And I looked up, and they were there.'

'I'm sorry, they?'

'The defendants. The Dunbridge team. They were there, and I knew that it was them that had left the … gooey substance on which … on which I was to fall … on.'

'For crying out loud,' Jenny groaned.

'She's not even a Hawk Falls girl,' Grace whispered. 'It's like people are just jumping on the bandwagon.'

'With the bandwagon being driven by *that* wagon.' Jenny glared across the aisle at Victoria's smug smile.

'It was a tapping sound – loud yet… yet quiet at the same time.'

The boy stammering on the stand had actually managed to work up a few tears. Grace couldn't believe it.

'And it obstructed your nightness?' Madame Three asked.

'My …' the boy stuttered. 'Oh, yes. Yes, it obstructed my nightness, absolutely. I haven't slept for days.'

'And how did you become aware that the guilty girls were to blame?' The boy stared at her blankly. 'Did you perhaps witness one of them, standing with their legs?'

'Oh, yes!' the boy said, smiling with brace-covered teeth. 'Yes, I woke up … no, I wasn't asleep … but I had my eyes closed, and then I opened them. And one of them was standing over my bed, banging on the wall with a … with a … they were banging with something, and I didn't see with what they were doing the banging.'

'It's like listening to a lobotomised goldfish,' Jenny said, slumping further and further onto the desk in front.

'And which of the guilty ones was it?' said Madame Three.

'Umm.' The boy's eyes moved across the faces of Grace and her team, apparently trying to pick one at random, but having trouble making a decision. 'Eh, that one.'

'What?' Adie gasped. 'That's not true.'

'You're only getting that now?' said Jenny. 'This here is what you call hysteria. And it's freaking hysterical.'

The tone of the trial was, indeed, working the spectators

up into a frenzy. The more ridiculous the so-called evidence was, the more witnesses came forward. Grace had stopped objecting to individual testimonies about five witnesses in. The girls had been accused of everything, from trying to poison the dining hall food with diarrhoea-inducing super-bugs (the canteen lady had been especially colourful in her description of green-faced students sprinting to the toilets. Grace had attempted to explain that the algae mash was capable of producing that effect with no additional help, but it had not gone down well), to pulling individual hairs from the arms of unsuspecting, and terribly traumatised, rival team members. The courtroom buzzed with judgmental fever, and all the girls could hope for now was that the enthusiasm would keep the witnesses coming long enough for them to figure out a plan of escape.

Lady Hecate banged the gavel once again for order.

'Are there any other accusers that wish to come forward?'

There were far too many *ooh, ooh, oohs* and *me, me, mes* from the crowd behind Grace, all accompanied by eager, upheld hands.

'In that case,' Lady Hecate said, again using the gavel for immediate hush, 'we will adjourn for the evening and recon-vene tomorrow morning.'

There was tutting and a chorus of *awwwws* from the disap-pointed mass that spilled into the hallway. From what Grace could tell, there had been no Witch Trial that day – the contest must be on hold while their own trial continued – which might explain the unwavering interest in their case. It was a good old-fashioned lynching, and the mob wanted a big finish.

The girls were led out by volunteer 'prison guards', students picked from the many who offered their services. Among them were one of the Raven girls, jet-black hair almost covering her beady eyes, a boy from Aura's team (poor Aura had winced at the girls in apology when he volunteered) and a frowning, tall boy with strawberry-blond hair.

'Gaukroger!' Adie whispered.

Her almond-shaped eyes shone when she noticed him. But he stayed facing forward and ignored her whispers. The gentle swell of bodies soon became jostling, and the girls were wedged in the double-doorway with every person in the place eager to get a look, sneer at them, even spit at them.

'Grace!'

Delilah's tiny body was being swallowed in the throngs of pushing limbs. Grace snatched her hand and pulled the girl to her, holding her around the shoulders as they almost toppled into further crowds in the hallway. She looked back; Jenny was digging her way through the mob, her arm clamped around Adie's waist, her jumper nearly stretched off one shoulder where Una held on fast. The prison guards were lost in the tumble and utterly useless.

'Grace, a few words.' Eder Verzerrt, short and nimble, had

wormed his way into the only space ahead. His notebook and pen trembled more than usual and he pinched his mouth to hide his smile of excitement.

'Eder,' Grace wheezed, 'help us out of here.'

He pushed his milk-bottle glasses up his nose as though he hadn't heard.

'Just a few quick words before you're returned to the Black Turret. Do you intend on rebutting today's accusations? Have you indeed deceived *all* in your quest for power? And where did you gain such power? Did you purchase Wiccan knowledge from a disgruntled banished master who turned to the Dark Arts to escape the never-ending cascade of depression and loneliness, with currencies stolen from pure-hearted witches whom you killed, leaving their bodies to rot in the bogle swamps for all eternity?'

'*What?* Eder, help us!'

'Don't take it with you,' he said in all earnestness.

'Take what?'

'The dungeons are forever, you'll never leave them.' He grasped her wrist. 'Don't take your story with you.'

Fury boiled inside Grace and she smacked the notebook out of his hand. Tightening her grip on Delilah, she forced her way through the crowd, shoulder-first, violently when necessary, until the mob thinned and she emerged at the other side.

'Going somewhere?'

Gaukroger stood in front of her. His tall frame, that had at first seemed awkward and ungainly, now loomed over her with square-shouldered confidence. Behind him the Raven girl grinned, her small eyes wicked in her long, oval face.

'Ow!'

Grace looked back. Jenny sprang out of the crowd, and Adie and Una lost their grip on her as she went sprawling onto the floor. Behind them Victoria Meister's hands crackled with blue energy.

'Nice guarding,' she sneered as Aura's team-mate snuck past her and joined Gaukroger and the Raven girl.

'We had it in hand,' Gaukroger replied coolly.

'Didn't you save their lives in Origination?' She smirked when Gaukroger scowled. 'Funny that. And three of them get away from you now? I think maybe you need to take a tougher approach.' She pointed a crackling finger at Jenny's back. 'A little encouragement will get this lot moving much quicker.'

'No!'

Una smacked her arm out of the way, and Jenny was able to scramble to her feet.

Rebounding off the mob that was moving steadily forward, Victoria snarled and snatched Una around the throat, pushing her against the wall.

'Behave, *dog!*'

Una whimpered as the blueness snaked up her neck and

144

reddened the skin along her jaw.

'Get off her!'

Victoria looked momentarily stunned as Jenny grabbed her collar and spun her away towards the opposite wall. They grappled and crashed into an ancient suit of armour. The two girls lay dazed in the scattered, dented pieces. It wasn't until Jenny sat up and shook her head that Grace noticed a gleaming sword was standing upright, its hilt leaning into the wall, its point lodged in Victoria's forearm.

'Oh no!' shouted Grace

The Hawk Falls girl slowly came to, screamed, and fainted again.

12

a wicked history

'I thought I could just talk to them,' Rachel said as she strolled along the gallery mezzanine.

'We don't like to communicate directly with Tithon Castle too often,' Alinda replied. 'We don't ... we like to keep some separation between ourselves and the Lyceum of Wicca. They school upcoming wiccans, and we are Wicca in action. We're two different worlds really. Are you not happy with your friends' letters?'

Rachel glanced at the pages in her hand. She wasn't happy with them. They were in her friends' handwriting, they used her friends' phrases but ... something wasn't right.

'They're all so upbeat, so happy.'

'Shouldn't they be?'

No, Rachel thought. *They shouldn't be. They're homesick, and nervous about the Trials.* But out loud she said, 'It's just funny. Jenny didn't make a single spelling mistake either, and she always makes one or two.'

Out of the corner of her eye Rachel saw Alinda tap a ruby ring on her finger. The red stone flashed for a split second, and when she glanced back at her letters she suddenly noticed an error in Jenny's writing.

'Oh,' she said, 'I didn't see that. Guess she did make one after all.'

She eyed the ring on Alinda's delicate hand and quenched the suspicion growing in her gut. When she looked up, the woman was smiling at her encouragingly. Rachel shrugged.

'I just hoped that I could talk to them, you know, ask them more about the Trials. I miss them, I guess.'

'Maybe I should explain a little of the history behind the Trials. You see, they're *nothing*.' Rachel looked up at her, perplexed. 'They're a distraction. What no-one outside this mansion knows, is that the Trials were created by the Hunters to weed out those that display enough skill to join our cause. The Glamour Trial is the only one that matters. Everything else is just distraction.'

'I don't understand. Then why not just have a Glamour Trial, and tell people what it's for?'

'Hundreds of years ago,' Alinda draped an arm around Rachel's shoulders, 'the Supremes were a force to be reckoned with. Did you know they've been alive that long? Well, they have. They were powerful witches with dreams of building a bigger, brighter future for all of us. They helped take control of this island. Before the Supremes and the Hunters arrived, faeries swarmed Hy-Breasal like locusts. Those three witches carved out a home for us here, and established the first formal school in the Lyceum of Wicca. Lord Machlau's gift for building and architecture made Tithon Castle the most glorious of its kind.'

Alinda's nostalgic smile faded and her voice grew serious.

'But the Supremes had their weakness. And that was greed. Not for money, not for power, but for *life*. They dreaded their own mortality, they didn't want to pass on. So they put their skill and knowledge into creating a potion, an elixir of youth. And they drank. Every day they drank, and every day they still do.'

'I can't believe they did all that,' Rachel said. 'They seem so, so—'

'Mad?'

'Well, yes.'

'That's because magic can stretch the lifetime of the body, but not the mind. We're not meant to live for centuries and the price for doing so has been their sanity. Lord Machlau can still remember every detail of the castle's construction, but he will never build another. Lady Hecate has held on best — she can curb the others' odd behaviour when she needs to — but she once had an astounding gift for potions that is long gone. And Madame Three, well …'

Alinda trailed off before continuing.

'Her dementia set in early, they say. You know she can't even remember her own name? And when she forgot it, so did everyone else. She's the third of their group, so they just call her Madame Three.'

'That's awful.'

'It is,' Alinda said. 'But it's a lesson to us all. When the Supremes tried to keep their hand in maintaining control of the island, it was disastrous. The faeries multiplied, and we're still trying to decrease those numbers. So the Hunters devised the Witch Trials. The preparations keep the Supremes occupied throughout the year, and over the decades they became a fixture at Tithon Castle.'

'So they get schools to send students to compete every year?'

'We absolved them of that responsibility – goodness knows what a disaster of organisation that would be – a perpetual spell was cast to pull in competitors from any wiccan school that qualified in any given year. Students can be pulled in at random, but generally a school selects those to compete and stands them ready to be summoned.'

'And to qualify a school would need … ?'

Alinda shrugged.

'It would simply need enough students to form a team.'

'Six?'

'That's correct.'

Delilah! Rachel thought, *Delilah was our sixth. She joined our classes, we qualified, and the spell sucked us in.*

'We have little contact with the Supremes now,' Alinda said, 'and we like to keep it that way.'

'But you still use the Trials to find new Hunters.'

'Our one indulgence, and it has served us well. We've found many talented new Hunters through the Trials. We found you.'

They moved down the spiral staircase to the marble floor below, and Rachel tried not to look at the paintings she already knew were there. Even in daylight the ground floor of the gallery was in shadow. Those eerie eyes – the blond boy with the wooden puzzle, the girl simpering from the cottage window with her fearful twin at the door – bored into Rachel while she gazed firmly at her feet.

'I come here once a day,' Alinda said softly, 'so I never forget.'

'Forget what?'

'Look around you.'

Rachel glanced quickly at the framed portraits lining the walls, then focussed on smoothing a hangnail on her finger. Alinda lifted her chin.

'You don't want to, but look carefully. Do you know who they are?'

Rachel shook her head.

'The Lost Ones. These witch-oags were the last victims of faery malice.' She pointed to the blond boy. 'Lark Walden, lured into the woods by nymphs, barely old enough to walk. He was never seen again. You see the girl at the cottage door? Vela Romwood; her story always gave me nightmares. She was snatched from the cradle and a sly, twisted creature was left in her place. It was not until the faery intruder revealed her wickedness as a teenager that the truth was realised. The real Vela was never recovered.'

They continued to the end of the gallery where an even larger portrait hung above an altar. Rachel hadn't seen it that night, because all her attention had been on the boy curled on the floor.

The painting had the same grim colouring as the others – all greys and blacks and dark greens – and depicted a cliff edge on a stormy night. A glowing lamp hovered in the air just above the ragged edge and a small boy, no more than two steps from his doom, reached for the lamp. His wore a white woollen nightgown, and his black hair was slicked to his forehead above huge green eyes.

'Tormey Vause,' Alinda said. She stared at the painting as if lost, and her voice dropped so low it was like she was talking to herself. 'Lured to his death by faery fire, held by the Phooka. Tormey saw the light in the forest from his bedroom window. He snuck out into the night and followed it through the trees, with the light always just out of reach.

151

He walked so far his feet were blistered, but faery fire has a strong hold. The Phooka, unseen, led him out of the woods to the very edge of the island and …'

Her voice drifted off. Rachel stared at the mournful scene, imagining the long fall into the raging sea.

'How do you know?' The words were out of her mouth before she had even thought them.

'I'm sorry?'

'How do you know the story?'

'These tales were handed down through generations so we would never forget.'

'Yes, but how does *anyone* know what happened? If the children were never seen again, how do you know the Phooka led Tormey to the cliff, or that nymphs lured Lark Walden into the woods? I mean, the Vela story maybe, but the others …'

She trailed off when she saw Alinda's expression. It was a mixture of disbelief and hurt. Rachel stammered an apology until the woman gently cupped her face in her hands.

'We know the truth,' she said earnestly, 'because the children will never let us forget. And we will *never* forgive.'

Again Rachel could feel the painted eyes glaring. The Lost Ones did not appreciate her lack of faith. She could feel it.

✷ ✷ ✷

Grace wasn't sure how she was climbing the long staircase

of the turret. Her whole body was numb. She could barely see in front of her, despite the light from the candelabra in the Raven girl's hand. She could feel Delilah's tiny hands in her back, guiding her up the steps. The small girl had prevented her from falling twice already. She tried to get her head together, but the scene outside the courtroom played over and over in her mind. The blood that spilled from Victoria's arm, the shock on Jenny's face and then, the sound of Madame Three's voice triumphant. The trial would continue as promised tomorrow, but with four defendants only.

Jenny was gone.

The turret door was unlocked and the girls pushed inside.

'Homey, isn't it,' said the Raven girl, 'but don't get too comfortable.'

'Because,' Gaukroger grabbed Adie's arm roughly and leered, 'you'll be joining your friend in the dungeons very soon.'

As the door slammed shut Grace slumped against a pile of rusted junk and began to cry.

'She's gone. *We're* gone. We're never going home.'

She looked up through a blur of tears and watched Adie turn towards her, shakily holding out the folded piece of paper that Gaukroger had pressed into her palm.

✻ ✻ ✻

The sheet of paper sat spread on the floor of the turret, a

sprinkling of what looked like pink salt over hasty, bubbled handwriting.

Rose myrrh, as much as we could find.

I hope it's enough.

Love,

Aura

And under the scribbled note was a shakily drawn diagram, marked with an X.

'I don't know what *rose* myrrh is,' Delilah said, 'but regular myrrh is sometimes used to break binding spells.'

'Then that,' Grace pointed to the diagram, 'is a map to the dungeons. Aura, you little angel.'

'Then he doesn't hate me,' Adie was whispering to herself, but the others heard her.

'Nah-ah,' Una said, squeezing her arm. 'That boy's head over heels.'

'He must be,' Grace agreed. 'They're risking an awful lot to help us.'

'Then let's not look a gift horse in the mouth. Let's look him right in the eye and … you know … accept the gift.'

'Let's do it!'

A few moments passed.

'Anyone know how to do it?' asked Una.

'Delilah,' said Grace, 'you know how to break a binding with the myrrh, right?'

'I know how to make a potion,' the small girl replied,

'with tools and other ingredients. I don't know how this stuff works on its own.'

'Careful, Una!' Grace said as her friend grabbed a pinch of the pink salt. 'There's hardly any of it.'

'We gotta try,' Una said, sprinkling the rose myrrh over the ring on her ankle.

Nothing happened.

'Abracadabra.' Una wriggled her fingers over her leg like a magician.

Still nothing.

'*Fudge.*'

✳ ✳ ✳

Aruj stood on the deck, broad-shouldered and handsome, his face turned to the high sun and the wind ruffling his loose-fitting shirt as the ship sped towards the forest. Rachel stared and tried not to drool.

'Are you nervous?'

She jumped, embarrassed that he was aware of her watching.

'I guess there *are* lots of faeries in the woods,' she said.

'There are. But you have no need to worry.'

'There was only one in the cell, and I didn't handle that well.'

It was the first time she had mentioned the tree-like goblin since it happened. She had been ashamed at how it

155

had ended, but much more than that, the experience had been one that gave her nightmares. Sometimes, sitting at the dining table or alone in her room, she would get the sudden sensation of sticky sap spilling over her hand and the deep smell of rotten wood. She shook her head to push away the dying hiss that hurt her ears.

'In my first training session,' Aruj said, still basking in the sunshine, 'I didn't even glamour. I sank into a corner before the Leanan-sidhe facing me, and I cried. But you, you fooled a black annis.' Rachel shook her head. 'You *did* fool a black annis, and took its life before it took yours. You achieved that in your first session. Just imagine what you will do in your tenth.'

Rachel sighed. Long before her tenth session Grace and the others would have found the sapphire rose they needed, and she would be back home, living her boring old life in boring old Dunbridge.

13

ALONE IN THE WOODS

Hours later Rachel was doing her best to keep up with Aruj. It was at this point in P.E. class that she would usually fake a stitch or ask to go to the bathroom, when the sweat would break out on her top lip and threaten to streak her foundation. She was so tired she didn't even try to keep an eye on the other Hunters that had melted into the woods around her. She wasn't the running type, and her tightening chest and wobbly legs were begging her to stop. It didn't help that the dense foliage blocked out most of the daylight, and she had to watch every footstep to avoid tripping over twisted roots and rambling vines.

And then she lost him entirely.

'Fudge!'

She looked left and right and listened hard, but the sound

of his feet were lost in the weird silence of the woods.

'Alrighty,' she said aloud to convince herself she wasn't scared, 'you're bound to run into one of them. These woods ain't that big.'

Saying *ain't* meant she was relaxed and casual, like a cowboy. And anything within earshot would know that. And the sun was already sinking and the forest was getting even darker. Why oh why did the Hunters always have to leave the mansion so bloody late in the day!

She took a deep breath and composed herself.

'Gonna head this way,' she said loudly, moving forward. 'Ain't nothing.'

After some distance, the sound of rushing water was welcome in the eerie quiet. Rachel sat on a rock by the stream and rested her weary legs. She blinked slowly and daydreamed of her warm bed in the yellow, silk room.

'Bringing together.'

Her eyes shot open and her blood ran cold. There was a woman right next to her, almost touching her, kneeling by the stream, hunched over a blob of soaked linen. She roughly rubbed the linen on a flat stone, grabbed one end, flipped it over, and rubbed it again.

'Bringing together,' she repeated, and Rachel thought she was talking to herself.

The woman didn't look at her; she was focussed on the washing in her hands, her black scraggly hair hanging over scrawny shoulders. Her cheekbones were high, almost level with eye sockets that appeared to be empty, just black holes in the parched face.

'Bring all together and take back the home.'

Rachel was frozen to the spot. If she moved at all she might touch the leathery skin and alert the woman to her presence, if she wasn't already aware of it. All she could think to do was glamour. The bogle was still fresh in her mind and, she hoped, so unthreatening that the washer woman would ignore her completely.

In her little grey body façade, she perched on the stone, absolutely still.

'Bring vampires and merrows and brownies and nymphs. Bring all together and take to the castle. Take to the castle and take back the home.'

'Take back the home.'

Rachel gasped. Opposite, on a flat stone across the stream was another washer woman, the same parched skin, the same empty eye sockets.

'Bring to the castle and take back the home.'

The women prattled on in rhythm and suddenly Rachel spied a third, further downstream, and another, and another.

'... to the castle.'

This one was just above her, kneeling on a larger rock, so close that the spray from her linen caught the back of Rachel's neck. They were all speaking in time together, but with differing sentences, like a chorus of *Row, row, row your boat.*

'Bring vampires and merrows and brownies and nymphs …'

'Bring to the castle and take back the home …'

'… take back the home. Bring all together and take back the home.'

'Bring to the castle and take back the home …'

'… vampires and merrows and brownies … and *bogles.*'

The woman in front of her had stopped washing. The leathery face was turned to her and the empty sockets stared. Rachel's own eyes stung with tears.

Don't move, she heard her own voice in her head. *Focus, and don't move.*

The others had stopped speaking. She didn't dare look away to see if they also stared at her. The silence went on forever.

'Bring all together,' she finally heard from a voice downstream.

One by one, the other women joined in, until the creature in front of her finally turned her face back to her linen and carried on washing.

✳ ✳ ✳

Light was fading on the sheet of pink salt. The girls sat, disgruntled, around the room, shivering against the cold wind that blew through the glassless windows. In the dimness, Grace could make out the scampering silhouette of the wood nymph at Delilah's feet.

He had eventually emerged from the birdcage after Delilah had opened the door for him, disappeared for a while, then returned to scurry about the small girl. Grace wanted him to squeeze through some opening and help them escape the turret, but he seemed only trusting of Delilah and stayed near her. He even played with her hair. To the others, he remained indifferent. In the evening light he looked like a pet rat flitting around her friend's ankles, and it gave Grace the creeps. She thought of Jenny, and what might await her in the dungeons, and she felt instantly colder.

The pink salt in the middle of the room teased her with freedom and the chance to save her friend. *If she could just work out how to use it.*

'No, no, get off it! You little rat, get off it!'

Grace snapped awake to the sound of Una's voice, and looked to the middle of the room in horror. The wood nymph crouched on all fours on the sheet of paper, chomping on the scattering of rose myrrh.

'Get off it!' Una took a swipe at him, but missed. He squealed, darting into the corner and vanishing into a crack in the wall. 'He's eaten all of it!'

Grace grazed her knees scrambling over the floor and looked down at the paper. Not a single grain left. If she could have thrown the little nymph from the window, she would have. They would never get out now. They wouldn't save Jenny. That little creature had just devoured all their hopes. In the corner she heard Adie cry afresh and Delilah sobbing in apology. But she couldn't comfort anyone else. It was too much, and she was too tired.

Tink tink tink tink.

Grace had fallen asleep on Aura's note. The paper stuck to her tear-stained face.

Tink tink tink tink.

'What?' Her eyes reluctantly opened.

Tink tink tink tink.

'What is that?'

She rolled over. It was still dark but she could make out the little nymph, his teeth stained pink with the rose myrrh, biting at the ring on Delilah's ankle. The small girl slept through the sound, curled on the stone floor.

Tink tink tink tink craaaack.

'Delilah!'

Her friend shot awake just as the ring clattered to the floor.

'He broke it,' Grace gasped. 'You're free.'

'Good work, little guy,' Una exclaimed, hurrying over to wriggle her finger in his face. 'Now do mine.'

The wood nymph clamped his teeth down hard on her finger, then scurried up Delilah's leg.

'Owww! You little rat, I'll—' Una took a deep breath, plastered a big fake smile on her face, and approached him again. Another bite.

'Ow! Delilah, make him break my binding.'

'I'm not sure I can. I don't think he'll do what I say.'

He wouldn't. Nearly half an hour of coaxing, and the nymph still wouldn't go near any of the others.

'This is hopeless,' said Grace. 'Look, we'll just have to work with what we've got. Delilah's got more spells under her belt than the rest of us put together, so this is still a pretty good result. We can work with this. I've got a plan.'

✳ ✳ ✳

'Tithon Castle,' Alinda said, her delicate fingers turning an hors d'oeuvre on her plate.

The post-raid buffet was a standing banquet of lusciousness, and was apparently only a precursor to the celebratory sit-down dinner that would follow. Rachel was trying not to fill up on the teeny tiny pastries that were so moreish, but her scare in the woods had left her belly grumbling.

'The castle is practically defenceless,' Alinda continued, 'and taking it would give the faeries a stronghold on the island. You said they planned to attack en masse?'

Rachel nodded, wiping flakes of pastry from her chin and

163

chewing quickly to swallow what was in her mouth.

'Yes, I think so. They said *bring all together and take to the castle.*' She took another pastry.

'Then it's certain. The gathering is for a coordinated attack, but not on the Hunters. On the Lyceum.'

'What?' Rachel stopped chewing. 'My friends are there.'

'As are many wiccan students,' said Aruj. 'We should have seen this coming.'

'By ostracising the Supremes we have left them, and everyone in their care, vulnerable,' Alinda sounded genuinely sorry. She looked firmly at Aruj. 'It is time.'

Rachel almost gagged in her hurry to swallow the last bit of hors d'oeuvre.

'Time for what?'

✹ ✹ ✹

Rachel shuddered beneath the drenched image of Tormey Vause. She knew she should feel compassion for him, and all the other painted children in the gallery, but the whole room made her skin crawl. She stood behind Alinda and Aruj as they carefully pulled apart a gilded box that sat on the altar under Tormey's portrait. A flash of movement at the other end of the room made her spin. Was that someone running? A child with black hair?

She looked to Alinda, breathless, but the woman had seen and heard nothing. Her focus was on an oval jewel in her hands. It was large, and deep orange-red in colour, and wrapped in twists of something that looked a mixture of metal and granite.

'Spessartine,' Alinda said, 'enfolded in orgonite. Older than anything you have seen or touched on Hy-Breasal, and still it shines like it is newly made.'

Aruj took the gem from her and held it up to the light.

'What is it?' asked Rachel.

'Our salvation,' the man replied.

'Thanks to you,' Alinda said, 'we know all the faeries of the island will congregate in one place. And with this, we can wipe them out in one fell swoop.'

All of them? Rachel thought of the little wood nymph from the birdcage; playful and harmless.

'How does that work?' she asked. 'Is it like a bomb or something?'

'Nothing so crass,' Alinda's voice darkened, and Rachel felt embarrassed for asking. 'This charm has been infused with magic for centuries, by hundreds of witches. Hold it and you'll feel its power.'

Aruj placed the orange stone in Rachel's hands and the heat pulsing from it warmed her palms.

'It was made by Hunters when they first took control of the island, and every generation has added to its store of energy. It was created as insurance.'

'Insurance against what?'

165

'Against a faery uprising, or any other disaster that could befall us. All the charm's potential is sealed inside the stone and, when it's needed most, can be released in one go with awesome effect.'

A bomb, Rachel thought again, but didn't dare say it.

'And it kills faeries?'

'If you want it to.' Alinda smiled.

'What do you mean?'

'The charm can be used for *anything*. Any desire, any attack, any defence, anything at all. But only once, and then its power is spent.'

'Like a wish. You mean you just make a wish. Whatever you want.'

'Yes, and your desire becomes reality. Even this charm could not wipe out every wretched creature on this island, but with them all in one place—'

'We can end the faery presence here forever.' Aruj smiled and gently took the stone from Rachel's hands, to her immense relief. It might not have been a bomb exactly, but the charm looked and felt ready to explode. She was sweating like a cop in some film, when faced with choosing between the red wire and the blue wire.

'Wow,' was all she could say to the other two. Pleased enough at her reaction, they replaced the charm with the utmost care.

Later that night, tip-toeing down the grand staircase

in the hall, Rachel buttoned her long-sleeved jerkin. She froze for a moment on the final step, thinking she heard a noise. She waited. Nothing. The mansion was silent. Creeping across the floor, she pulled back the iron bolt and slunk out the door.

She trusted that Alinda and Aruj's plan was sound, but it did mean waiting for the faeries to mass on the castle, and she couldn't risk her friends getting hurt before the Hunters unleashed their magical nuke. She had to warn them.

The cold night air bit at her skin. It was very dark, with some little light from the moon, but the green hue that layered the island during the day was still obvious. It made the landscape in front of her look unreal. She had considered trying to fly to Tithon but she didn't have the stamina for that kind of distance. If she were to drop out of the sky halfway and weak from the effort, she'd be done for. No, she'd have to walk it and glamour her way through the woods if need be.

She hurried through the grounds, past black and silver flowering bushes that made the place look like a graveyard, and through the small door in the massive gates. The stretch of barren land ahead didn't worry her – she could see anything coming – but the woods beyond were dense and full of creatures she didn't want to meet. But she had no choice: she had to go through them. To go around them would triple her journey time. Taking a deep breath, she pulled her jerkin tighter and started walking.

Behind her, a pattern followed on the fissured rock. Wet footsteps left by invisible feet.

14

escape to the Library

Grace was losing the feeling in her legs but was too anxious to move. She sat on the stone floor of the turret, her knees pulled up and her arms wrapped around them. *When three moons have set.* The Ferryman's words kept echoing in her mind. Moonlight drifted across the floor; the third moon was passing.

Delilah had been gone for ages. The tiny girl had safely glided from one of the tower windows to the wild-grown grounds below. The others had watched her creep into the building, and hadn't heard or seen anything since. The night was running out and they had a boat to catch.

Suddenly, there was a *c-clunk* of a key in the lock, and the door swung open. Grace's heart leapt when she saw Delilah in the doorway; the tiny wood nymph was perched on her shoulder, with Gaukroger and Aura standing behind.

'We have to hurry,' Aura said urgently. 'It'll be sunrise soon. Come on.'

Grace pushed Una ahead of her, starting down the spiral stone steps. Behind her she heard Gaukroger's voice, low and serious.

'I'm sorry about before. I had to—'

'Thank you.'

Grace snatched a glance back, and saw Adie smile and take his hand.

'You can hide in the library until morning,' Aura said, taking furtive looks up and down the corridor when they reached the bottom of the stairs. 'Then sneak out when everyone's in the dining hall. You don't want to go now; you don't want to be outside the castle walls in the dark.'

'We have to get to Madame Three's room first,' Grace said. 'There's something there we really need.'

'That's crazy,' Gaukroger said. 'What do you need from Madame Three?'

'A blue rose. It's … it's hard to explain.'

'We need it to get home,' said Adie. 'It's payment for the Ferryman.'

Gaukroger's face fell. 'Then it's true.'

'We're not bad people,' she said, taking his hand again. 'We didn't even want to come here, we just got sucked into the Trials.'

170

'Literally,' said Una. 'Down a chute.'

'We never meant to cause any trouble. We just want to get home.'

Gaukroger looked to Aura, and the little girl shrugged gently.

'Alright,' he said. 'Then let's get you your rose.'

'What about Jenny?' asked Una. 'We've got to get her out before we leave.'

Aura looked frightened and shook her head.

'She's in the dungeons,' Gaukroger said gently. 'She's gone.'

'No,' said Grace. 'If there's a way in, there's a way out. We'll get the rose, we'll get Jenny, and we'll get out of the castle in time to make the ferry.'

'We can't help you get into the dungeons.'

'That's alright,' Adie said. 'We'll find our own way. You're doing too much for us as it is. And don't worry,' she gave him a comforting smile, 'we're good at getting out of a pickle. It's what we do.'

Keeping to the shadows, they skirted along the walls, and raced to the safety of the library.

Una lay on the check-out desk in the library, bouncing a rubber ball she had found off the wall. Grace flinched every time it hit the flaking plaster.

'Knock it off, Una. Someone'll hear.'

'Don't distract me,' Una said, her focus on the ball, 'I'm up to ninety-eight, ninety-nine, one hundred. A hundred and one– Hey!'

Grace caught the ball mid-air making Una scowl. She looked around for Adie who had disappeared into the maze of bookshelves with Gaukroger. Her friend had seemed so keen when he mentioned his favourite titles. Grace smiled to herself; Adie had never been enthusiastic about books before.

'Here,' Aura had been rummaging in a narrow cupboard behind the desk. 'I knew they had one left.'

She handed Grace a black slate, like the ones she had given them before.

'Oh that's okay,' Grace said. 'I don't think I could handle seeing my mum right now.'

'It's not a home slate,' the young girl replied. 'It's a prope plate.'

'You're going to have to help me out there.'

'A *prope* plate. You can use it to see how Jenny is. Because I don't think …' Aura seemed to reconsider, and reached for the black shard. 'Maybe it's not a good idea.'

'No, no! It is. Thank you.' Grace held it out in front of her. 'How does it work?'

'Holding something personal of hers, you've to imagine yourself inside her mind, and spit on the plate. Just be careful; these ones crack like glass. We've never got any at Balefire, they all get broken in the first term.'

'Cool. Here, Jenny gave me one of these.' Una pulled a thin, leather bracelet from her wrist and, before Grace could stop her, leaned forward and spat all over the plate. Grace wiped some stray spit from her eye.

'You've still got your binding ring on, Una.'

'Oh, whoopsie.'

Una handed Delilah the bracelet, and the tiny girl closed her eyes for a moment, then spat neatly onto the black slate. Nothing happened at first, then there was the smell of burning, the spit evaporated in wispy smoke, and a dim image blurred into view on the stone.

'I don't understand,' said Grace. 'I don't see Jenny.'

'You're seeing through her eyes,' Aura replied. 'This is what she sees.'

Grace's heart sank. Giant green-moulded slabs made up the walls of the dungeon, decorated by rusted rings with thick, corroded chains hanging between them. Squares of faint light from far above slightly illuminated the gloom, and Grace could hear steady drips of water landing in puddles across the floor.

'There's sound,' she said, her voice cracking.

'We're close enough to hear.'

'Oh, poor Jenny!' Una gripped Grace's sleeve, then harder still. 'What's that? In the corner, in the dark.'

Two flecks of yellow blinked in the dusk of the room, narrowed, and blinked again.

'Hello?' the girls heard Jenny say. 'Is someone there?'

There was no answer, but Grace could hear breathing.

'Hello?' Jenny's voice again, anxious this time.

'Who is it?' Una snapped at Aura. 'Another witch? Someone dangerous?'

'They haven't thrown anyone into the dungeons for decades, as far as I know.' Aura replied. 'But—'

'But what?'

'But I've heard it's where they kept captured faeries, from way back. From when the castle was first built.'

'But they'd be dead by now,' Grace said. 'That's so long ago, they'd be dead. Of old age, right?'

'Some faeries live for a few years,' Aura said, shaking her head. 'Some for decades, some maybe for centuries. They're all different.'

Grace snapped her attention back to the plate, where the yellow eyes grew rounder and a husky voice laughed in the dark.

✵ ✵ ✵

Rachel stood at the edge of the woods, listening to the gentle rustle of the wind through the leaves. Once she stepped through the trees, though, she knew that weird silence would cloak everything. She wriggled her fingers, playing with the buzz that moved up and down her knuckles. Her safest bet was to glamour herself now, and become

174

just another faery moving through the forest. She wanted to be something small, out of sight, but the vegetation sprouting from the woodland floor was high in places, and she needed to see where she was going and what was coming towards her.

She built up the buzz and rippled her fingers down her face. Asrai was a faery she had studied in the *Faery Encyclopaedia* – tall and lithe, it was a creature that stayed near water and loved the moonlight. It was cover that would only work before the dawn though; Asrai melted in direct sunlight.

She would find the stream, follow it to the river that curved around the woods and, from there, she would be able to see the castle. Standing tall, with silver hair that spilled to her waist, she stepped into the quiet.

Her own footsteps were the only sound she could hear. Before long the fireflies came, pairs of white light that blinked in the bushes. *The nosey ones,* Alinda had called them. Faeries that watched passersby in silence and sometimes, if they were unlucky, scared them for fun. Rachel was alarmed at how many there were, but these ones seemed just to be watching. And watching.

She found the stream by the sound of rushing water, but cringed at the memory of the washer women. She hoped she wouldn't see them again. She followed the stream as it wound its way through the woods. She hopped over rocks and climbed down when the water tipped over a small fall, spraying cool mist on her face that kept her alert. She was getting close, she could feel it.

But Rachel's good luck couldn't last. Straight ahead, a blue-skinned creature sat hunched on the bank. It was only half her faery-size, but she knew it was some kind of water sprite, and they were capable of bending water to their will. The wings on its back were actually large, delicate fins that cut through the water, making it a swift swimmer.

'Good evening, asrai.'

Rachel jumped with fright. The creature had its back to her.

'Good evening, sprite.'

With that polite greeting she hoped to be on her way, but the sprite raised her face to the moon and turned a little for more conversation.

'And so you go to gather?'

The creature's deep set eyes were huge in its small, oval face. The irises were a deeper shade than its skin, and even the whites of her eyes were pale blue.

'You cannot fight in sunlight,' the sprite continued. 'And yet you go to gather.'

Rachel didn't answer, and the blue faery took that as confirmation.

'I waited here among the fireflies, but they speak only nonsense. I long for conversation and for ...'

'For what?' Rachel dreaded the answer.

It was long coming.

'For *hope,*' the sprite said finally.

Shaking a shower of droplets from her long fins, she suddenly leapt from the bank, slipping her hand into Rachel's and smiling.

'And so I will go with you to gather.'

She took off at a run, dancing over the ground with beautiful grace, pulling Rachel behind her.

Time was short. Grace tucked the prope plate into her waistband and tried not to think of the yellow-eyed thing that cackled at Jenny in the mouldy dungeons. All the girls could do was watch, and that didn't help anyone. They would split up – Gaukroger would take Adie and Una to Madame Three's room, Grace and Delilah would travel into the depths of the castle and rescue Jenny – with as much direction as Aura could give them. They slipped out of the library, with the young girl on point.

'There,' Aura pointed down a corridor without windows, and unlit by candelabras. 'I don't know how far it is, but somewhere down there is the entrance to the dungeons.'

'Thank you, Aura,' Grace said, squeezing her hand. 'Adie, Una, you sure you're alright with your part?'

'It's no biggie,' Una said, hiding her fear with a smile. 'Gaukroger's gonna show us Three's room, we nip in, get the rose, nip out, Bob's your uncle.'

'Rendez-vous point is the Closet.'

'Right you are. See you there.'

Grace gave her friends as confident a smile as she could manage, then turned down the dark corridor with Delilah. The nymph had taken to squirming inside Delilah's shirt, just under the collar. It gave the girl a little hunchback that looked eerie in the duskiness.

Behind them, in the distance, there were the sudden sounds of a scuffle. A sudden cry from Adie made Grace's stomach lurch.

Racing back to the mouth of the corridor, they hid behind the corner and watched, in horror, as Adie and Una grappled against the six members of the Hawk Falls team, plus the Raven girl who had been their guard. Aura slipped into hiding in the shadows.

'Checked the turret myself,' Raven girl said. 'I told you they were on the run.'

'Real stealthy, *Raven*.' Gaukroger walked towards them as if he had just arrived, gripping Adie's arm and keeping as stern a face as he could muster. 'I've been following these two so they'd lead me to the others. Guess we'll just have to forget about catching their little friends now, won't we?'

The Raven girl blushed, while Victoria Meister pushed through the group, her arm swaddled in potion-stained bandages.

'Where the hell are the rest?'

'They can't have got far,' her purple-haired friend replied.

'We should keep these two safe for now.' Gaukroger's cheeks were reddening as he spoke, and Victoria watched him suspiciously. 'The Supremes will go mad if they haven't got someone to try this morning.'

'Fine,' Victoria said sharply. 'Raven and I will take them back to the turret, while you take everyone else to find the others.'

Gaukroger gave Adie a pained look, doing his best to steer the group in the wrong direction. At least he would keep them well away from the dungeon passageway.

'Come on,' Grace said, grabbing Delilah's sleeve and pulling her back into the darkness. 'There's nothing we can do for them. We'll get Jenny first, then go back for Adie and Una.' She sighed. 'Guess it's all up to us now.'

The small girl nodded, her big eyes wide and worried, and she followed Grace down the sloping floor to the dungeons ahead.

The ground, that at first had been a gentle incline, became steeper and steeper, until Grace and Delilah had to lean back with hands on the wall to keep their purchase on the damp floor. The corridor had grown like the dungeon walls, slippery with green mould.

'We'll fall,' Delilah said, her little hunchback squirming with nerves, 'if this gets any steeper.'

'You'll have to fly,' said Grace, 'and guide me down. Can you do that?'

'I'll try.'

Delilah closed her eyes in concentration, then hovered off the floor. Gripping hands, the girls travelled deeper into the murk, Grace putting more and more weight on Delilah as her feet slid in front of her. The floor dipped further.

'I can't get a grip,' Grace gasped, her legs bicycling. 'I'm going to fall!'

'Just don't let go!' Delilah yelled as Grace hit the ground and skated downwards, dragging the small girl with her.

They shot down the passageway, picking up speed until the ground disappeared and they were in free-fall. Grace screamed as she waited for the ground to come up and smash her, but Delilah dug her fingers into Grace's hand, slowing their dive before they finally hit rock with a thump. Grace landed first on one knee and her chin, an awkward angle that sent a spike of pain down her back.

'Delilah,' she groaned, her eyes adjusting to the gloom, 'you okay?'

'Yeah,' a voice replied with the shuffling of someone trying to get to their feet. 'I'm alright.'

'And your little friend?'

'He's okay too.'

'Thanks for slowing the fall, I think you saved my face there.'

'No worries.'

Grace squinted as she looked up but couldn't see the entrance to the passage.

'We're gonna have a rough time getting out of here,' she sighed.

15

a gathering

It was cold underground. Ahead of her Delilah shivered, and Grace squeezed her fingertips in her hands trying to drive out the freezing numbness, but the damp drove the cold into her bones. She grimaced. The little wood nymph didn't seem bothered by the frigid air. He scuttled in and out of Delilah's collar, backcombing her long, black hair, and took regular perches on top of her head.

'Bllliiingg-lo!' he'd exclaim, pointing ahead, then scurry back under her collar, only to pop out again.

They had followed the only source of light but, reaching a junction of corridors, realised the green glow was actually bioluminescent algae spreading over the mouldy walls in patches. There were three possible routes and, at the end of at least two, Grace could see even more passages.

'It's a maze,' she said despondently. 'How are we ever going to find her?'

'One passage at a time,' Delilah said firmly. 'I can leave charm stars so we can find our way out of each one, but they won't last. We'll have to hurry.'

'Hold on,' Grace said, pulling her woollen jumper over her head and moaning as the cold cut through her thin t-shirt. 'Let's go for something more permanent. Ever hear that story about the Minotaur and the Labyrinth?'

Delilah scrunched up her face, thinking, then smiled as Grace tore at the knitted fabric with her teeth. After pulling a few loose strands from the hem, she finally managed to drag out a long thread, and began to unravel as much of the jumper as she could. Delilah took hold of the wool as she worked, and tied it tightly around the pointed ends of a fractured stone in the wall.

'*Couno*,' she whispered, running her fingertip over the loop of thread. The cream thread melded into the stone as if it had grown there. 'So it doesn't move,' she said.

'Excellent.' Grace grinned. 'Let's go.'

'Should we go left, right or straight ahead?'

'You choose.'

Delilah took a deep breath and walked straight ahead, until the little nymph zipped to the top of her head, stretching up as tall as he could go and grasping tiny handfuls of her hair.

'*Blllinnng!*' he squealed.

183

'Ow!' Delilah rubbed her head. 'That hurts.'

'What's up with him?' said Grace.

'I'm not sure. Wait a minute.'

The two girls stood silent, waiting as the nymph jammed his nose in the air and sniffed and sniffed. Finally, with one long last *ssssnifff*, he pulled the handfuls of hair taut again and yipped,

'*Blllinnng-lo Yo!*'

'Ow,' Delilah moaned, jerking her head to the right. 'I think he wants us to go that way.'

'Do you think he can smell Jenny?'

'He can smell something.'

'Well, right is as good a direction as any. Let's go.'

With the wood nymph steering with Delilah's hair like reins, they went deeper into the dungeons, leaving a line of cream wool in the green light of the glowing algae.

Rachel sat quivering under her glamour. The murmuring and shuffling of so many bodies covered the occasional whimper that escaped her lips. The blue sprite sat next to her like a child, bored with waiting. Her legs were pulled up to her chin and her azure arms rested on her knees. She huffed now and then, peering down the sloping woodland to the centre of the commotion, then dropping her cheek impatiently onto her arms again when there was still nothing to see.

The crowd of curious creatures had gathered around an enormous mushroom with a cap that might once have been red. Its huge head leaned to one side, straining the groaning grey stalk that supported it, nearly touching the ground. It was pitted and scarred and darkened by age, and shiny streaks of liquid ran from the newest of its wounds. It was obviously important to the faeries, sacred even. Rachel could tell because no matter how raucous or swollen the crowd became, the creatures never spilled into the grassy area surrounding the mushroom. They all kept a reverent distance.

There were faeries as far as she could see, packed around a clearing in the trees shaped like an amphitheatre. More water sprites, their skin in varying shades of blue and green, hopped delicately in and out of the stream that cut across one end of the slope, grasping at the tentacles of ferocious-looking merrows that had dragged their muscular bodies upstream from the river. Rachel shuddered as one looked her way, bearing the razor-sharp teeth that lined the mouth of his elongated snout, but he turned to snap at a bright green water sprite, shaking his mane of tentacles in fury as the snickering sprite leapt out of his reach. Pixies, wood nymphs and brownies flitted among the feet of larger faeries, and there were numerous other breeds that she didn't recognise. To her alarm, another asrai caught her eye from across the clearing, smiling warmly. Rachel returned the

185

smile but quickly looked away. She had to keep clear of her and any other asrai, just in case.

'It's too close to home,' she heard Aruj's warning words in her head. 'A faery will usually recognise its own breed. And will easily reject that which is not.'

There was a loud *ffft ffft* sound and the crowd was silent. The huge mushroom groaned as something inside it moved and the large cap swung slowly from one side to the other. One of the old wounds was splitting apart and long fingers, like the legs of some giant cellar spider, pushed through, tearing at the fungi flesh. Both hands came free, then clamped either side of the split as a long head squeezed out of the narrow hole. Rachel was reminded of the time she was allowed to watch lambs being born in the field next to her house. She tried not to gag.

In the art room, back at school, there was a print of a famous painting called *The Scream*. A long, oval face, screaming in the picture, was surrounded by wavy lines of orange and blue that made Rachel feel nauseated whenever she looked at it. She didn't like the painting. The screamer's face was distorted and the eyes stared. It made her feel uneasy. But she remembered it clearly now because the fungi faery's face was just like that.

The creature sat on his hunkers atop the giant cap now, like a cat about to pounce. His legs and arms were long and skinny, like his fingers, and his torso resembled a crooked toadstool stalk, pitted and grey like the mushroom he emerged from. He opened his mouth to speak, stretching the jaw first and slapping his tongue noisily off his palate, as if it hadn't been used in years.

'Centuries in exile from our own lands.'The words sloshed out of his mouth like water from a bucket. 'Forced to cower in the depths of the forest for humble relief.'There was dead silence as he spoke. 'But no more. At dawn we take to the castle, and take back the home.'

There was an eruption of cheers and clapping. The fungi-like creature waited patiently for the crowd to settle. When it finally did he stared for several moments at the ground, his shoulders sloped and his pale face the picture of sadness.

'This was our home once, for so long. And we lived full lives, for so long.'

He went quiet again and Rachel was sure someone would hear her heart thumping in the stillness. When the fungi creature lifted his face, there were dark grey streaks running down his face.

'So many of you are too young to remember. But some of us remember. The balance of this island was broken, and my heart broke with it. But today I will mend my broken heart, as we will mend our broken home. There will be lives lost, but those ghosts will fortify the good spirits of the island and restore harmony. Either way,' he raised his voice and one hand in the air, 'you will go *home.*'

Another explosion of cheers and wild clapping. Rachel joined in, feigning enthusiasm, while the blue-skinned sprite nudged her arm with excitement.

'Follow the stream to the river by the east end of the forest and wait,' the fungi faery shrieked over the commotion. 'We attack at dawn!'

'What can you see?' Delilah said, wincing as the nymph pulled her head back to face front. 'Is she okay?'

Grace balanced the prope plate uneasily on the base of her thumb, the fingers underneath working the thread free from the jumper in her other hand. With so little light she could barely make anything out.

'I don't know,' she said. 'She hasn't moved her eyes from that spot.'

The scene on the slate was exactly what she had seen in the library. Jenny was staring into the dark at the back of the cell.

'Ssh, stop for a sec!' Grace said suddenly, freezing. 'Do you hear that?'

That rasping, low laugh was growing again. Jenny's view snapped up and down as she looked for the source of the sound, but the bare stone made for endless echoes.

'Have they left you down here?'

The voice was coarse, with a mocking falsetto that made

188

Grace break out in a sweat despite the terrible cold.

'Have they left you down here,' the two yellow flecks appeared, 'for *me?*'

'Wh– who's there?' Jenny's voice trembled. 'Who are you?'

'You know who I am.'

Grace could hear the smile in his voice. The prope plate wobbled on the edge of her hand; she spread her fingers beneath it to keep it steady.

'I don't know who you are,' Jenny whispered. 'I don't know who you are, and I'm not here for you.'

'Hmm,' the voice groaned, 'are you chained to the wall?'

Grace suddenly realised she was; why else wouldn't Jenny have run?

'They left you down here,' the voice went on. 'And now you're all alone. With *me.*'

The face that shot out of the dark made Grace's throat tighten in panic and, before she could stop it, the black slate toppled from her hand and smashed on the stone floor. She stared at the broken shards, tears streaming down her face.

'No!'

'What was it?' Delilah hissed. 'What did you see?'

It was an animal's face, not a human's. The head of a goat, a hood of dark brown, shaggy hair covering a bony face and spreading over broad shoulders. Two thickly ridged horns twisted from the top of his skull, and his yellow eyes were without pupils, staring and hideous.

189

'I can't … it was …' Grace shook her head and appealed to the wood nymph. 'We have to find her. Little man? We have to find her. Look at me!'

The little nymph paid her no attention, but Delilah reached up and tapped him swiftly on the back until he resumed his rein-pulling.

Grace tugged at the sorry remains of her jumper. There was still some wool to go, but the unravelling thread was caught. She tugged again, roughly, and the thread snapped.

'Fudge!'

She tore feverishly at the jumper with her teeth, ripping out more thread, but the remaining material bunched as she pulled and the threads snapped.

'It keeps getting caught in itself,' she said, her hands shaking. 'I don't think we'll get any more out of it.'

'We'll have to leave it here,' Delilah replied, 'and hope that we see it on the way back. I think we're close. He's getting all worked up.'

If she hadn't been terrified out of her wits, Grace might have laughed. The nymph was practically dancing on top of Delilah's hair, which was now backcombed into a halo around her head.

A few more turns and the little nymph was near hysterics. He hissed through his teeth, yanking on Delilah's hair until she threatened to put him in her pocket.

'Shh!' Grace said suddenly, ducking down and dragging the other girl with her. '*Listen.*'

There was that voice in the dark, just around the next corner. It was still mocking, threatening in tone. But at least he was still talking.

'Of course you do. Children-shaped and filled from the bowels of the island. Frauds and fakery keep the masses subdued and all the while … all the while…'

In the following silence, Grace and Delilah edged closer and closer to the turn in the passageway. Then the voice sounded again.

'My heart is black and burnt. These rings have cut my wrists a thousand times, and they will a thousand more. Tell me … do you feel safe? Do you think you're safe?'

Suddenly the nymph leapt from Delilah's head and scurried around the corner. Delilah reached for him but missed and, as she turned to give Grace a questioning look, there was a cry.

Jenny.

The two girls scrambled around the corner and faced an open cell. To their right Jenny kneeled, her wrists fixed to the wall with rusted iron rings, her head slumped forward as she cried. In the back of the cell, straight ahead, stood something tall and broad. He took one step forward, gently moonlit by a skylight far above, and Grace recoiled in horror.

The creature stood upright, his goat's head perched on a seven-foot frame, his dark mane matted and straggled with dirt and damp around his twisted horns. He was also fixed to the wall, but by two lengths of chain. He had room to move – and just enough chain to reach Jenny.

'You were watching.' The yellow eyes swivelled and fixed on the two girls. 'But what did you see?'

He moved one cloven hoof and Delilah fired a burst of silver stars as Grace grabbed a loose hunk of stone and fired it at his head. Stooped and snorting, he didn't see the rock that struck him and knocked him back into the dark.

'Delilah!' Jenny gasped. 'Grace, no!'

With another loose stone Grace attacked one of the rings on Jenny's wrists, clanging and chipping away at the rusty metal. She worked furiously, ignoring Jenny's shouting in her ear. They could talk when this was over and she was free. She glanced to her left and saw Delilah hold her palm over the other ring, mumbling under her breath with her eyes closed. Like fast-growing lichen, the rust spread under her spell, eating into the metal, making it weaker and weaker. Grace's arm ached as she slammed the rock on the ring, over and over. It was working. The ring was dented and flaking and, beneath it, her powerful blows were chipping at the stone wall that held onto the metal. Something was going to give.

'*Grace,*' Jenny's voice rang out under the constant clash of stone on metal, 'listen to me, it's–'

'Nearly there! Just hang on.' There was a dull crack and the rusted metal split. 'Yes! Got it.'

Grace wrenched apart the jagged ends of the split and freed Jenny's hand. Her right wrist was still bound, but Delilah's magic was gradually turning the ring to brown dust. Just another minute or two and they could run. But the growl from the back of the cell gave them no time. The goat-headed beast lunged from the dark, meeting Grace nose to nose as she pressed her back against the damp wall. Delilah clenched her fist and kissed her fingers, ready to throw more silver stars, but Jenny knocked her arm away.

'Stop!' she said. 'You mustn't do that.'

The goat beast was so close, Grace could feel the cold as he inhaled, and the heat as he released each irate breath. The yellow pupil-less eyes were so inhuman.

'He didn't hurt me,' Jenny said, putting a calming hand on Delilah's clenched fist. 'He told me where to get drops of water from cracks in the wall when I was parched. He could have hurt me if he wanted. He didn't. I think … it's okay, he's not dangerous.'

Grace wouldn't believe her. Those soulless eyes were bad, she was sure of it.

'Break the ring, Delilah.' Her voice was level, and she never took her eyes from the goat beast. 'And then we're leaving.'

The goat laughed his raspy laugh.

'And how will you get out?'

'We've left …' Grace started. 'We can find our way out.'

'Find the entrance maybe, but your foot is circled like your friend's.' He nodded to the binding ring on her ankle. 'Will your small friend carry you both?'

Grace could feel Delilah's gaze on her. They both knew she wouldn't be able to carry either of them back up to that awful slanted corridor. Grace still hadn't taken her eyes from the goat.

'We'll find our way out.'

He smiled, knowingly, but backed off and gave her room.

Delilah resumed her powdering of the metal ring, and soon Jenny's wrist was free.

'He's right, you know,' Jenny said out loud, to Grace's dismay. 'It took three of them to take me down that black hole and lock me up. Delilah can't manage it alone.'

'We'll find a way.' Grace knew her repetition was proving nothing, but she was determined not to look afraid. 'Come on, let's go.'

'Maybe …' Jenny said, hesitating. 'Maybe we should let him go.'

'Absolutely not.'

'Grace, he's been down here for centuries. Wouldn't you be a bit strange after all that time alone? He's not–'

'He's a faery!'

'So?'

'Rachel said they're dangerous. The Hunters kill them – all day, every day – they spend their whole lives taking out faeries because otherwise …'

'Otherwise what?'

'Look,' Grace said, exasperated, 'they're dangerous, alright? All of them.'

'What about B-brr?' Delilah said.

'Who?'

'The wood nymph.'

'You called him B-brr?'

Delilah put her finger between her lips and went *b-brr, b-brr, b-brr.*

'He does that,' she said to Jenny, who was giving her a queer look.

'Well, he's not …' Grace struggled to get the words out. 'He's too small, I guess, to be dangerous.'

'He broke my binding ring,' the small girl said. 'He showed us the way to Jenny.'

Grace sighed. She couldn't bad-mouth Delilah's pet. Without him, they would never have escaped from the turret or found Jenny. *Little rat still ate all the rose myrrh,* she growled to herself.

'Fine, he's okay then. But we can't set the goat-thing free, Jenny, we just can't. We don't know him, and we can't trust him. I'm sorry.'

'Phooka,' the sing-song voice said from the back of the

195

cell. 'I'm the Phooka. And you don't have to set me free.'

He stepped from the dark, all seven feet of him, and held his arms up to the light. His wrists were bare, and his chains lay in a heap on the floor. At his feet, the wood nymph grinned up at the girls, licking his lips, his teeth still pink with the stain of rose myrrh.

16

THOSE OF THE darKness

Rachel picked her way through the dark forest, still shaking with adrenalin. Far to her right, she saw a pale body disappear into the trees, the last faery within sight. As the mass had moved from the clearing, she had veered away from the stream, getting further and further from all the others. The blue sprite had followed her for a time, but she managed to lose her by ducking into some bushes when the sprite was momentarily distracted. She would emerge from the woods much farther from the castle than she had hoped, but she would be out of sight of the faery gathering at the eastern edge.

There were no firefly eyes watching this time, and she

told herself that she was finally alone; except that she felt she wasn't. She couldn't hear anyone in the unnatural silence that plagued the woods, but she moved as lightly as possible, breathing quietly, as if to hide herself from him or her or it, whatever it was that was following her. There was a rustle of leaves behind. She spun around and caught a glimpse of something white, maybe with black hair. A little boy? Her mouth was so dry it hurt.

'You're a long way from home, little asrai.'

She felt her eyes widen in shock. Right in front of her, the fungi creature hung from a branch, his pale face like a mis-shapen moon in the trees.

'And dawn approaches.'

She backed away, stumbling on legs that felt like jelly.

'Yes,' she gasped. 'It's nearly dawn and I should go.'

The screamer face smiled weirdly.

'I do admire the moon faeries. You have an elegance never quite equalled by your daylight friends.'

Rachel continued to move backwards, too terrified to turn, but the fungi faery crawled swiftly from the tree towards her. Standing upright he would have been taller than she was, but his knees remained bent and his body hunched. She couldn't bear the sight of his long bony fingers, and was forced to stare at his face instead.

'You know the stories, little asrai,' he said. 'They've told you.'

She was frozen to the spot and didn't dare speak.

'How three witches found a haven in the sea; an island of plenty, filled with magic and beings of every kind. How they were welcomed with open arms, given leave to make their home. But the witches were greedy, they would not share. Their greed unsettled the spirits of the island, strengthening those of the darkness, and leaving those of the light weak. There was no longer balance. And our kind fell. It is a tragic story, is it not?'

She nodded her head.

'I wish you no harm, little asrai,' he tilted his head sadly, 'though I fear you cannot say the same. The dark spirits hold sway over more than just the ground beneath your feet; they poison weaker minds, planting seeds of malice and revenge. But I have hope that your mind is yet free.'

Rachel sucked in a shaky breath as he leaned up close enough to whisper in her ear.

'Beware what has followed you from the grand house, and do not trust your eyes. Innocence is the greatest disguise.'

He sank back onto bended knees and smiled.

'Good luck, little asrai. I wish you all the best.'

Rachel watched the Fungi walk slowly eastwards on his odd bended legs. She dropped her glamour. What was the point? He knew what she was and he'd let her go. He must have presumed that she would tell the Hunters of his plan, but he made no effort to stop her. Was he telling the truth about the three witches? Did the Supremes really steal the island when they had the choice to live freely among the faeries?

A sobbing sound made her turn and she realised she had been standing rigidly the whole time, like a statue. A shock of black hair poked out from behind a tree and a little white hand grasped the bark. Slowly, the ghost of Tormey Vause crept into view. His huge green eyes were bloodshot with tears and his face was stricken with fear. Rachel shivered in sympathy at the sight of the small, cold child in a drenched nightgown. He looked so defenceless.

'Don't let him get me,' he whispered.

Rachel shook her head.

'He's not going to hurt you. No-one can hurt you.'

'Don't let him get me,' the boy repeated, his pale skin tinged blue with the cold. 'Don't let the faery get me.'

He stepped towards her and Rachel instinctively stepped back.

'He led me to the cliff,' he said. 'His wicked faery light led me to the water.'

'The *Phooka*,' Rachel replied, narrowing her eyes. 'Alinda said the Phooka led you to the cliff.'

There was a pause and the little boy shook his head slowly.

'The fungi faery led me to the cliff. You must kill him. Kill him and save me.'

'Kill him!'

Rachel jumped at the sound of another child's voice to her right. Lark Walden stood there holding his colourful wooden puzzle. He looked too young to understand what he was saying, but his huge eyes looked up pleadingly under his blond hair. Some feet away stood Vela Romwood, her skin and clothes the grim colouring of her portrait. All of the children – and more had appeared – had that strange colouring; too grey and too bleak to be real.

'Kill him,' they echoed. 'Kill him.'

Rachel shook her head, trying not to look afraid.

'No,' she said firmly. 'I don't believe you. I won't help you.'

The echoing stopped but the children remained staring. She stepped between them; they made an eerie guard of honour as she moved forwards, avoiding the glaring, foreboding eyes. When she was out of sight of them, she told herself, she would run.

Rachel's limbs were weak with exertion and terror. She couldn't run anymore and she was too tired to glamour. She was as vulnerable as she could be in these woods, but all she could think about were her friends in the castle. They had no idea what was coming, and she was the only one who could warn them.

Her vision was becoming blurry with fatigue, and the growing mist curling around her ankles wasn't helping. She leaned against the black bark of a tree, blinking against the tiredness and trying to revive her senses. Up ahead, through the fog, she could see some warm light. Had she reached the edge of the woods? It must be daylight and, despite what dawn would bring, she felt comforted. Following the yellow glow she found a small break in the trees and there, hanging in the air, was an amber lamp.

It was like a mini-sun hovering in the night-time. She closed her eyes and basked in its light. It was warm and soothing and it eased the aching in her limbs and the worries on her mind. But it moved, taking its warmth with it. She frowned, and followed it, taking a u-turn back the way she had come. If she stayed within a few feet of it she felt that serenity that sunshine gave. Any further than that and the cold night air brought back her pain and anxiety with a shock. So she followed it; back into the woods, and further from her friends in Tithon Castle.

Grace ignored Jenny's attempts to delay the rescue mission. Her friend could be bossy again when they were out of the dungeons; down here, she was in charge. She clenched her friends' hands even tighter, making Delilah wince in pain, and ploughed ahead.

That little rat, she thought to herself. *All that time he was chewing on those chains and setting the Phooka free.* She wished she had thrown the wood nymph from the turret window when she had had the chance.

She didn't waste a second when she saw the goat creature was no longer tethered to the wall. She had snatched her friends by the hands and pushed them out of the cell. Now they were running at full pelt through the dark passageways, scouring the stone floor for that sad bit of cream jumper. Her heart was sinking, believing she had dragged them the wrong way, but *there*! There was so little of it she almost missed it in the dull green gloom.

'Got it!' she cried, letting go of the others and clutching the material.

'Did you guys leave that here?' Jenny asked, impressed.

'Grace's jumper,' Delilah replied. 'So we could find our way back out.'

'Clever.'

'Come on,' said Grace. 'We've gotta move. If the little rat could follow the scent to your cell, he can follow ours to the entrance. We need to run.'

She ran ahead, gathering up the thread as she went. The others followed. They made it back to the first junction, and looked helplessly at the spot where Grace and Delilah had landed with a bump.

'Any ideas how to get out yet?' said Jenny.

Grace grimaced. She hadn't any.

'Climb,' she said at last.

'That's impossible.'

'Maybe not.' Grace pointed to the cracks between the stone blocks. 'Use these for hand and foot holds, and Delilah can hover behind us to catch us if we slip.'

'The walls are slimy,' Delilah said. 'You *are* going to slip.'

'Both of us,' Jenny agreed. 'We're both going to slip, and Delilah can't catch two at a time. Even one of us would drag her to the floor. One bad fall and someone's going to break a leg.'

'That would be a terrible thing,' said a raspy voice behind them.

The yellow eyes glowed. The girls backed into the wall beneath the entrance high above. They were trapped. They couldn't climb, and they couldn't run past the tall, horned figure that blocked the passageway.

'Since you were banished to the dungeons, little witch,' the Phooka said to Jenny, as the wood nymph scampered about his hoofed feet, 'and these two came to your rescue, I presume that none of you are welcome guests in the castle above us.'

There was an audible gulp as Jenny shook her head.

'Then you have no allegiance to the Three?'

'The Supremes?' Jenny said, 'No, no we don't.'

'Well,' said the Phooka, coming close, 'I am glad.'

He crouched down and wriggled a little, as if in pain. The girls gasped in horror as two protrusions erupted from

204

his hairy back, stretching and bursting the skin. There was no bleeding, but the protrusions lengthened and unfolded, revealing a pair of feathered wings, each the length of his whole body. When he lifted his head, the goat's face with its shaggy brown hair was gone and, in its place were two round, bright eyes and an expanding beak of a shiny grey colour. The cloven hooves were now taloned feet, and a wave of dark gold feathers ruffled from his neck to the top of his head.

'The enemy of my enemy is my friend,' he said in a lighter, sing-song voice. 'Climb on, little witches.'

The great bird turned to one side and lowered a wing. The girls looked to each other.

'Can't be worse than trying to climb,' Jenny whispered. 'I think we'll have to take a chance, Grace, I really do.'

The girls climbed on, each gripping a handful of feathers for balance. With a sudden jerk they were airborne. Within seconds they had reached the slanted corridor and crawled off the Phooka's back, relieved to be on solid ground.

'The little rat still likes you then,' Grace said as the wood nymph perched on Delilah's shoulder gripping her ear with one hand.

'B-brr,' the small girl said.

Grace gave in.

'Fine. B-brr.'

The nymph jammed a finger between his lips – *b-brr, b-brr, b-brr* – then beamed at Grace with his pink teeth.

Yeah, still don't have to like you, Grace thought.

'Adie and Una,' Jenny said. 'Are they still in the turret?'

'We think so.'

'They were grabbed before they could get to Madame Three's room and get the sapphire rose,' said Delilah.

Watching the Phooka's transformation from eagle to goat was one thing, but Grace winced at the bone-groaning sound of those wings pushing back into his body. Looking up at his long face under the twisted horns, she couldn't help wishing he would remain a bird.

'More friends imprisoned,' he said, smiling. 'My, my, you have been naughty.'

The Phooka backed away into shadows without another word. His grin was the last Grace saw of him, and it sent a shiver up her spine.

✷ ✷ ✷

The fog was thinning and Rachel could make out the cliff edge and the sound of rushing waves below. Now that she was clear of the trees, the rain stung her face and urged her closer to the comfort of the amber light. She reached out to touch it and it moved nearer to the precipice. If she could hold the light, she need never be without that warm feeling again. If she could just grab it. She stretched again, the lamp jerked out of her reach, and the sound of the sea got closer.

Her feet moved from spongey grass to emerging rock and she knew she was close to the edge. But it didn't matter. All that mattered was staying close to the light.

In the distance, along the coast, she caught a glimpse of a pebble beach.

The Ferryman.

For a split second her stomach twirled in panic; was she about to go over? *But it doesn't matter,* she told herself. *Just stay close to the light.*

Then out of nowhere, thoughts of her friends filled her mind. They were in danger at the castle. They needed the Ferryman to get home. They were trying to get to that beach with the sapphire rose so they could pay him. She looked past the amber light to the hint of red sky that promised sunrise. Her friends needed her. They were in *danger.*

She took a step back. Pain shot through her arms and legs, and she was suddenly terrified. She clenched her teeth and took another step away from the edge.

'It's cold,' a voice said beside her.

Tormey Vause stood like his portrait, soaked and pale on the cliff edge.

'It's cold,' he said again, shivering. 'Stay close to the light.'

Rachel didn't move.

'Aren't you very cold?' he asked.

She nodded and bit her lip.

'The light will keep you warm.'

207

Grace, Una, Jenny, Adie, Delilah. Rachel saw their faces at the forefront of her mind. As the little boy put out his hands to stop her, she turned away from the lamp, walked right through his ghostly form, and ran back into the woods.

17

THE SAPPHIRE ROSE

Hunters' ships. Four of them. Rachel could see them skimming along the barren landscape in the last of that night's moonlight. The last half hour had been a blur. She didn't know how she'd raced through the dense woods, barely aware of her surroundings, when her body was ready to drop with exhaustion. Her detour to the cliff edge had cost a lot of time, and there was no way she would cover the distance before the faeries advanced on the castle. But, from the direction of the Hunters' Mansion, she saw the cavalry. Four ships, sailing at full speed, could take her directly to her friends. But only if she could get their attention.

They moved fast, eastwards towards the castle. They were some distance from her and it still wasn't morning. They would never see her.

Think, she said to herself. *Think, before you lose them.*

She needed a signal, something to catch someone's eye. Could she light a fire? Frantic, she looked around for some dry bits of wood she could rub together to make a flame.

What the hell are you doing? she thought. *You're no freaking girl scout and there's no time!*

She sighed and looked down at her feet.

Flame.

Flame-running.

She could light a fire with her *feet*.

She was shocked at how much it took out of her just to rise into the air. With sweat already breaking out on her brow, she started running, hovering on the spot. She pedalled and pedalled, her breath coming out in gasps and wheezes. Her legs hurt. They were tired and sore and wanted to stop, but she kept running. Her head was light and fuzzy; coloured spots drifted into her vision.

A spark!

But not enough. Still no flame. The weariness oozed through her limbs like liquid lead, threatening to drop her to the ground. The desperation came out in a flood of tears.

'Come on!' she screamed at herself. '*Come on!*'

Another spark, and this one took. The blue flame swept from her heels to her toes.

'Now, *move.*'

She obeyed her own command, and plunged her head

forward, leaving a trail of fire in her wake. She made as long a trail as she could before the parched earth swung up into her bleary vision. Everything went black.

✳ ✳ ✳

She awoke on the solid floor of a ship's deck. Alinda brushed the hair from Rachel's face and, behind her, Aruj looked on, concerned.

'What were you doing out here all alone?' Alinda said.

'The … faeries,' Rachel struggled to clear her fuzzy mind, 'they're–'

'Gathering by the eastern edge of the forest,' Aruj interrupted. 'We know. Since you saw the *mnathan nighe* we've had Hunters undercover, but the beasts were all too wary; we couldn't find out when the gathering was to take place. Then a scout by the river saw the commotion an hour ago.'

Rachel looked past him to the morning sky.

'It's dawn!' she gasped. 'They were to attack at dawn.'

'Movement west of Tithon Castle,' someone shouted from the bow. 'They're swarming!'

Alinda and Aruj disappeared from her view, and Rachel rolled awkwardly onto her front to get to her feet. There were far more Hunters on the ship then had been on the scouting party days ago, and she had to push her way through leather-clad bodies to reach the others and look out over the helm. In the distance, the faeries did look like a swarm. She thought of the Fungi and his words of warning.

'Alinda,' she said breathlessly, 'listen, I think this is a mistake. That nuke, that mega-wish thing, you can't use it.'

Alinda's gaze was fixed on the army charging towards the castle.

'So many of them,' the woman whispered.

She looked frightened. Rachel grabbed Aruj by the shoulder and swung him around to face her.

'This isn't right,' she said firmly. 'This feud, this war ... whatever it is, I think it's all fake. Tormey Vause, Lark Walden, the Lost Ones, none of them ever existed. You and the faeries can share the island, there's no need to fight.'

'You met something in the woods?' He gently gripped her shoulders. 'You should never have gone there alone. They manipulate and twist the truth, they play games with your mind. Whatever creature led you astray, they lied to you.'

'But it was Tormey Vause who led me astray.'

There was sudden silence on the deck. Rachel felt nervous now that all eyes were on her.

'You saw the Lost Ones in the forest?' Alinda gasped.

'Yes! And they tried to lead me off a cliff. They're not children, Alinda, they never were. I think they're the dark spirits of the island. The Supremes knocked the spiritual balance out of whack or something, by trying to take the whole place for themselves. The light spirits got too weak and the dark ones got too strong. And the dark ones have been able to keep it that way by convincing you that the faeries are all evil, and that they kidnapped innocent children and all sorts.'

Alinda looked as though she'd been kicked in the stomach. Rachel was flustered now, and conscious of the suspicious glares directed at her. She wasn't sure she was being as articulate as she could be either. Still she ploughed on.

'I mean, did any of you personally know anyone who knew the Lost Ones when they were alive? I mean, I know it was centuries ago, but aren't any of them from any of your families?'

There was no answer.

'Shouldn't some of you be related to some of them some way?' persisted Rachel. 'Or did they just pop out of the blue?'

'We all know the suffering of the Lost Ones,' Alinda said.

She had recovered. Her voice was low but assured.

'Because who told you? Them? Their ghosts? I've seen them too, but I know they're not what they say they are. Please, Alinda …'

The distrustful look in the woman's eyes made Rachel feel uneasy.

'Aruj?' Rachel looked to the handsome face for support, but he also looked wary of her now.

She was suddenly aware how dangerous her position was. If she wasn't careful, they would suspect her of trying to help the enemy, even of being a spy. The Hunters surrounded her, each with a hand on the hilt of a sword, and the silence stretched uncomfortably in the fresh morning air. Rachel decided on drastic action. She shook her head, putting a hand to her eyes.

'I ...'

She shook her head again and swooned, slowly enough for Aruj to step forward and catch her.

'I ...' She looked up as if seeing him for the first time that day. 'Aruj? I ... I don't know what's ... That fungi faery, he told me something, but I ... I don't think it's true. My head feels all cloudy. Where are we?'

'Heading for Tithon Castle,' he replied, 'and a great battle.'

She looked directly into his eyes.

'The faeries. They'll kill my friends,' she said.

'Yes.'

She pushed herself out of his arms and stood firmly on the deck.

'Then let's kill them first.'

The tense atmosphere dissolved and the Hunters spread out through the ship once more. Alinda looked to Rachel with pride and relief, and Rachel faked a smile in return. She had bought some time. If she could change the fate of the faeries and witches, she would. But her friends came first.

✳ ✳ ✳

Shoulders pushed past Grace as she slunk against the wall. It was early morning when she and Jenny had finally emerged from the sloping corridor that led to the dungeons, and they had expected the halls to be empty. They were anything but. Students from all schools elbowed and kneed their way through the packed passageways, everyone frantic to be somewhere else.

But not the same somewhere. The panic was not in one direction; it made the shuffle so much messier that the streams of human traffic were headed all over the place. The only good thing about this was that no one seemed to care anymore about the two filthy humans squirming their way through the crowds. Delilah had taken the little wood nymph in the opposite direction, en route to the Black Turret. Grace hoped she would get Adie and Una out okay.

In the rush, she grabbed a boy by the elbow. He looked terrified.

'What's going on?' she asked. 'Where is everyone running to?'

'They're coming,' he gasped. 'They're coming to kill us all.'

'Who's coming?'

'The faeries. Didn't you know? They're coming from the forest. Hundreds of them.'

'Thousands,' a girl said, tugging at the boy's other arm. 'No, *millions*. Millions of them and they're going to overrun the castle and kill everyone, and we're all going to *die*!'

She pulled the boy from Grace's grasp and headed off

in a different direction to the one they had been going in. It was complete chaos.

'You!'

Grace and Jenny spun around to see Victoria Meister, her eyes red and scared under her short, blonde hair. She pointed at them, her sleeve pulling up to reveal the bandaging on her arm.

'You did this. You brought the faeries here.'

'I've been in the dungeons, you twit,' Jenny said. 'Where *you* put me.'

'Seize them!' Victoria cried to no one in particular. 'They're the ones who called the faeries to the castle.'

She was ignored. The panic continued as bodies jostled around the three girls.

'Seize them!' Victoria cried again.

Grace felt a twinge of pity. The girl looked helpless and afraid, her pointing arm shaking and her frightened eyes darting left and right as she looked over the crowd. The lifeless sable swung as she turned, its dead legs slipping from her shoulders. Her world was falling to pieces around her, and she was all alone.

Grace looked to Jenny, who nodded, and they pressed on through the hordes. As they left her far behind they could still hear Victoria's voice crying out.

'They're getting away, stop them! You, stop the humans. They brought the faeries down on us. We're all going to *die*!'

Two turns after the dining hall, they were climbing a spiral staircase. It was part of the Summerland Wing – where the Supremes' rooms were – and was pretty much a dead end. It was practically deserted – nobody wanted to get caught on a floor with only one exit. More than halfway up the stairs was a narrow window. In the early morning light Grace could see a dark mass advancing from the woods.

'It's true,' she gasped. 'And there are hundreds of them.'

'We've got to move,' said Jenny. 'Or we'll never make it to the beach in time.'

At the top of the stairs they reached a short corridor. There were torches fixed to the wall on one side, but their light had little effect. Black oozed between the cracks in the stone and the air felt heavy, oppressive, like a weight bearing down on them.

'This place is bad news,' Jenny groaned. 'Like *really* bad.'

'Then let's not stay long.'

There were three doors. The first, on the left, was polished mahogany, with a geometric border burned into the wood. Next, on the right, was an oak door, solid and undecorated except for a tiny, corked bottle where a knocker would be. The glass was clear, and there was nothing ornate about the bottle. The final door on the left was white ash, but didn't sit easily in the doorframe. The wood was warped so the curved top leaned out of the doorway, and several long cracks split the length of the door. Grace took a deep breath and felt

Jenny's hand on her back as they pushed this door open, the misshapen timber scraping over red tiles inside the room.

Straight ahead, a messy four-poster bed with tattered lace hangings looked like it hadn't been made in years. Next to the bed was a chaise longue, stained and mouldy with age, and a dresser with porcelain figurines that were draped with swathes of dense cobweb. Around the corner, the room opened into a much larger space, and Grace recognised it instantly. At the far end a huge snow globe sat, filling the space from floor to ceiling, and it looked like the only cared-for item in the room. Its silver base shone like it had just been polished, and the glass was crystal clear and without a single smudge.

Madame Three was hugging the globe, her arms pressed against the curved glass. On a table next to her sat a decanter of sparkling yellow liquid, and a small cup. She seemed oblivious to the girls' presence.

'We're out of time,' she said softly, 'but don't worry. They'll not take you. I've always kept you safe and we will be together forever.'

Inside the globe, the exquisite silver statue stood with her arms outstretched; at her feet lay the sapphire rose. Grace stared at the blue flower that was her and her friends' ticket home.

'Madame Three,' she said. 'The castle will be under attack in a few minutes. You need to leave while you still can.'

'I am happy here,' the woman replied.

'No, you don't understand. The faeries are coming–'

'From the woods, where we chased them.' She looked up from the globe with a nostalgic smile. 'I didn't forget it all, you know. I remember the best of those times. I remember them running and screaming and crying. We had so much power, and they were too trusting.'

Grace didn't like the look on the woman's face.

'We took it all and we chased them into the woods,' Madame Three went on. 'And we built a big castle and we were going to live forever. We took it all and everyone was so impressed. Everyone, except,' her fingers traced the glass, '… her.'

The light was fading from the woman's eyes and Grace rushed to keep her talking.

'Who is she?'

The eyes lit up again.

'The girl of silver, the silver hair, the silver eyes, the silver skin …'

Her voice trailed off and Madame Three's eyes closed.

'Who is she?' Grace asked again, louder.

'My love,' the woman replied, her eyes reopened, watery with tears. 'But she wouldn't come with me.'

'Go with you where?'

Madame Three glanced at the decanter on the table.

'To forever.'

'What do you mean?'

'Heccy saved the day. Mixed up the yellow potion so that we would live forever. Me and Heccy and Machlau and her, we would all live forever. But *she* wouldn't do it.'

She looked mournfully at the silver woman and Grace inched her way forward. She looked into the face of the statue and was startled when the light grey eyes moved.

'She … she's alive!'

'And with me always,' said Madame Three. 'I'll keep her with me always.'

'You *trapped* her in there?'

Grace's horror was cut short by the muted sounds of screaming from the floor below.

'They're here!' Jenny said. 'We've got to leave. *Now.*'

She kicked the table, sending the decanter flying. Madame Three howled, throwing herself to the floor too late to catch the flask before it smashed to smithereens, the yellow liquid spreading over the tiles. Jenny picked up the table and swung it hard against the snow globe. The glass cracked.

'No!' Madame Three screamed, scrambling to her feet.

Grace leapt onto her back, holding her down while Jenny swung a second time and the glass shattered. The statue began to shudder like there was an earthquake just beneath her feet. Silver leaf curled off her arms and legs until her joints were free and she slipped forward onto her knees. She took deep breaths as Madame Three wailed beneath Grace's weight. The final scraps of silver fell from her tragic face. But what happened next made Grace's legs go weak.

The young woman revealed beneath the precious metal began to age. Crows' feet spread from her eyes and her skin softened and sagged. Her fair hair turned grey and then white, and the flesh on her limbs shrunk. She was now an old woman, but the ageing continued. Jenny stepped back, dropping the table, as the woman looked up at her.

'Thank you,' she whispered.

The words were barely out of her mouth before her lips shrivelled and pulled up over her gums. Her skin darkened almost to black and the remaining wisps of white hair drifted to the ground. Her whole body dried up like soil in the sun and her hands, still outstretched, started to crumble to ash.

A few seconds later, nothing was left but a pile of dust.

Madame Three clambered out from underneath Grace. She scooped up handfuls of the ash that spilled through her fingers and moaned. Jenny stepped through the broken glass and grabbed the sapphire rose.

'Come on,' she said to Grace. 'We're running out of time.'

Grace was unable to tear her gaze from the woman kneeling in the ash on the floor, until Jenny gripped her by the collar and pulled her to her feet.

'Come *on*.'

✶ ✶ ✶

Halfway down the staircase Grace glanced out the narrow window. Throngs of faeries filled the castle grounds. They were all shapes, sizes and colours, and buzzing with the excitement of the attack.

They haven't got in yet, she thought. *Everyone still has a chance.*

A sucking sound drew her gaze directly below. Webbed, deformed hands latched onto the stone wall like blobs of glue. The thing's grotesque face, with a tongue so swollen it spilled out of its horrible mouth, grinned up at her like it was starving and she was a ready-meal. She scanned the rest of the wall. There were dozens of them, climbing like lizards, growling and slurping and heading for the arrowslit windows.

'They *are* going to kill everyone,' Grace said. 'They're all around the castle and they're nearly inside. What are we going to do?'

'The dungeons,' said Jenny. 'Get everyone to the dungeons and they can hide out there. And then we've got to find a way out to the beach, okay Grace? No waiting around to see if everyone makes it.'

'I know, I know. I don't want to miss the boat any more than you do.'

18

into the dungeons

'Aura! Aura!'

Grace heard Jenny's breathless shout as she barged through the crowd in the corridor. The passageways were darker now. Many of the windows on the lower floor had been barricaded against the lizard-things that slithered up the outer walls of the castle, but she had passed more than one staircase that was also piled high with furniture. The creatures were coming in through the upper floors and making their way down. All the better for her and Jenny's plan to work; the students were being herded into a smaller and smaller area. All they needed was a push towards the dungeons.

'Aura!' Jenny's voice sounded again.

Grace had fallen behind, pressing her way gently through the mass of people, cradling the delicate sapphire rose beneath

223

her jumper. It was a pretty thing, with blue petals of such finely cut gemstone she didn't know how it didn't fracture into pieces in her hands. When Aura caught up with the two girls and grabbed them, Grace instinctively twisted away to protect the flower.

'Did you see those creatures?' the little girl said, her eyes wide and scared. 'The creepy ones with their tongues hanging out. They were climbing the walls, getting in the windows. Did you see their faces? They're going to eat everyone.'

'They're not,' Jenny said. 'Because you're going to get everyone into the dungeons.'

'If we go down there, we'll *never* …' Aura looked to Jenny as if suddenly realising. 'You got out of the dungeons.'

'Piece of cake when you're not chained to the wall.'

The passageway to the dungeons was at the east end of the castle, and the flood of people was accumulating there, being farthest from the wall under attack. The air was thick with panic and the howling of terrified kids who were now trapped and waiting for the slaughter to begin.

'Gaukroger! At last!' Jenny cried. 'We thought we'd never find you.'

The tall boy looked aghast at the girls.

'You're free! How did you–'

'No time to explain,' Grace said. 'You have to help us get everyone into the dungeons. They're sitting ducks up here.'

'Are you serious?' he exclaimed. 'They'll never go down

there. *I* won't go down there. Once you're down there you ne–'

'Never get out,' Jenny finished his sentence. 'Yeah, we've heard that before, but we've been down there and we made it back, no bother.'

'It's a labyrinth down there,' Grace said. 'There's plenty of space to hide, and only one entrance. You can keep it guarded. Trust us, Gaukroger, this is the only way.'

A sudden shriek and Grace looked up to see a lizard faery dangling from the ceiling, His swollen tongue hung from his mouth, dripping dark saliva. There was a flurry of bird's wings, and an ebony bird twice his size snatched the faery from his perch, its beak pinching closed around his arm. Grace spied the Raven Hall girl who had volunteered as prison guard, her face fixed in concentration. A vicious roar burst from the faery's thick throat, and he grasped the raven's cheek, biting down hard. They grappled, torn feathers showering the crowd below like confetti. Grace shuddered at the strength of the lizard-thing – its limbs were thin and lithe – it should have been no match for the bird. But they continued to struggle and, eventually the bird took off through the corridor, with the lizard faery still attached to her head.

'Into the dungeons. *Now!*' Jenny began pushing people onto the sloping corridor.

Aura had found Arick and two other members of Balefire Warren and, with their help, the crowd began to move reluctantly towards the opening at the end of the passageway.

There was a sudden explosion of animals – birds, dogs, cats, insects – as the wailing and crying students crammed into the gloom. Grace ducked as a miniature dragon caught its claws in her hair.

'No companions!' she yelled. 'There's no *room*.'

She clutched Gaukroger's arm.

'Tell everyone, no companions up here. They can originate something to guard the entrance once they're down there but, until then, no clogging up the corridor.'

The boy nodded, and began passing on the instruction. There was a slow and steady series of pops as the companions were dismissed, but the frenzy continued. The smaller kids were panicking, slipping down the stones as the incline got steeper. Those that could hold it together enough to hover did so, catching and guiding those that were too frayed to help themselves.

Grace watched the blackness of crushing bodies slowly disappear down into the dungeons, and relief loosened the tension in her shoulders. Just a few stragglers remained now, tearfully quibbling with Gaukroger as he explained their predicament in calm, reassuring tones. Aura was just ahead of him, her little feet just off the ground as she helped lower the last of her charges to Arick below. She looked back at Grace and Jenny, raising her hand and blowing a kiss, before descending gently through the cavity in the floor.

'Goodbye, Aura,' Grace whispered, blowing a kiss in return.

They were all gone now, save for Gaukroger who stood at the halfway point between them and the dungeons, looking back expectantly. Grace knew who he was waiting for, but there was no time. She opened her mouth to tell him as much, when Una's shrill voice came thundering towards her.

'Grace! Jenny!'

There was a whoosh of a short, black bob, then Grace was slammed against the wall, Una's arms squeezing so tight that the sapphire rose bit into her stomach.

'Ow, ugh! Hey, Una.'

'Hey yourself.' Una backed off to give Jenny a bear hug too.

'Where's Adie?'

'She's coming. Look, there she is.'

Delilah was rushing towards them and, behind her, Adie followed, apparently without the jeans she had been wearing when taken to the turret. Luckily, she was also wearing a long knitted sweater that stretched nearly to her knees.

'Where are her pants?' Jenny asked Una.

'Tied to a bed frame by the window,' Una replied. 'We couldn't get the knot open.'

'Adie, why did you tie your pants to a bed frame?'

'It was an escape plan,' Adie said sheepishly. 'We were trying to make a rope to climb down.'

'With your *pants*?'

'It was *all we had*,' Una exclaimed with her hands held wide. 'Anyway, we can pick her up a pair in the Closet on the way out. Aren't we leaving now? Delilah said there's a bunch of faeries coming to eat our brains.'

'Yeah, we're leaving,' Grace replied, looking up in trepidation at the sound of scurrying lizard-bodies emanating from the floors above.

She was turning to go when she noticed Adie had quietly padded down the corridor to Gaukroger. The tall boy grasped Adie's hands and tipped his forehead to hers. He leaned in to kiss her lips.

'Move it or lose it, Adie!' Una roared. 'It's cold outside and you've got no pants on.'

'Una,' Grace said softly, 'maybe give them a minute.'

'They can do that relationship stuff later. We're on a schedule here.'

'What if this is all the relationship they'll ever have?'

Una thought for a moment. 'Adie, you take your time,' she yelled. 'I'm gonna get you some pants.'

'Smooth,' said Jenny.

'Thanks. You coming with?'

'Delilah, can you go with her instead?' Grace said. 'You're the only one with fire power.'

'Sure,' the small girl replied, and she and Una trotted away.

'Be careful!' Grace called after them. 'And don't waste any time. Get to the hallway by the front door as soon as possible and we'll meet you there.'

When she turned back, Adie's arms were wrapped around Gaukroger's neck as they kissed. Grace blushed and looked away.

'Hate to be a party-pooper,' Jenny said quietly, 'but Una had a point. We've gotta get moving.'

Grace nodded. She felt bad, seeing Adie squeeze her eyes shut as she rested her head on the tall boy's chest, but the castle was filling with horrible beings that would soon be swarming the ground floor.

'Adie?' she called gently. 'It's time.'

Adie's almond-shaped eyes opened sadly and she pulled back, gazing up into Gaukroger's face. He smiled his wide smile, kissed the tip of her nose, and they separated, their hands touching for as long as they were in reach. Adie walked clumsily up the corridor backwards, not taking her eyes off him.

'You ready?' Grace said as she reached them.

'Yeah,' her friend said with a sigh.

When they looked back down the corridor, he was gone.

'One pair of pants for one loved-up lady.'

Una held out a pair of navy, thick-ribbed corduroy trousers and Adie curled her lip.

'Are they *drawstring*?'

'We were in a hurry – these were in your size and looked warm. You're *welcome*.'

Grace thought Adie must have been relieved to say good-bye to Gaukroger before this particular garment found its way into her ensemble. She didn't even have to take her runners off to get them on; they were almost bell-bottoms.

'See?' Una looked triumphant as Adie tied the drawstring at her waist. 'Like a glove.'

The girls had regrouped just outside the Closet after all, some way from the reception hallway. The thumping upstairs had gotten louder, and there was the definite crashing of furniture as faeries smashed through the barricades at the bottom of each staircase.

'They're on this floor,' Grace said suddenly. 'I don't think we're going to make it to the door!'

As if on cue, something black and spindly sprang from around the corner and jumped on Adie. It grabbed handfuls of her hair and threw her towards the wall. Adie gasped and curled up against the creature that perched on her side as she lay on the ground. It wasn't a lizard-faery. Its limbs were splintered and pointed, like broken branches, and its triangular mouth grinned at the girls with sharp, yellow teeth. It crouched into Adie, ready to spring again.

'Delilah!' Grace yelled. 'How do we–'

Slam.

The sound was dull and dreadful. Jenny stood panting, the

sword she had pulled from the suit of armour adorning the wall behind them was still in her hand. She had hit the gremlin with the flat of the blade and he was out cold.

'God, Jenny,' Una breathed. 'If you'd hit him with the sharp bit his head would have come right off.'

Grace didn't want to think about it.

'Let's go,' she said.

But more crashing up ahead told them this was just the first of many creatures in their way.

'They're everywhere,' Adie whimpered, her eyes streaming. 'We'll never get through.'

Grace stood listening to the echoes of the castle that now seemed full. Adie was right.

'I've got an idea,' Delilah said, grabbing one of the long, mauve curtains that framed the window overlooking the arena. 'Help me.'

The others gripped the material and pulled, jumping up and down until they heard the crack of breaking mortar, and the curtain rail came loose and plummeted to the ground. They leapt out of its way, then Delilah tipped the rail up and shook the curtain rings off.

'Everybody under here,' she said, pulling the heavy velvet over her head like a hood.

She whispered under her breath and was instantly cloaked, an empty space where Delilah had been.

'Eh, we're still really visible,' Una said. Grace nudged her.

They remained quiet, listening to the small girl as she continued whispering. Slowly, the material above Delilah's invisible body began to disappear. Within seconds the entire curtain was a giant invisibility cloak, hiding everyone beneath it.

'You've got some skills, Miss Gold,' Jenny said with a grin.

They shuffled as one down the corridor, but five people (and one little wood nymph) moving together beneath a shield of velvet was cumbersome. There had appeared to be acres of material when the curtain was hanging but, with all of them beneath it, there was barely enough to mask them all.

'I'm not covered,' Adie rasped. 'Una, you're pulling it off my shoulder.'

'That's 'cos Jenny keeps getting under my feet. I can't see where I'm going!'

'None of us can see where we're going,' Grace said sternly.

'I can,' said Jenny. 'The material's worn a bit here. I can just about see out.'

'Right then, you're our eyes. Adie, you hang on to Una, I'll hang on to Delilah, and the two in the middle hang on to Jenny. Got it?'

'No,' said Adie, 'I'm still–'

'*Shh*,' Jenny hissed, ducking down so their velvet cloak skimmed the floor. 'Something's coming!'

It wasn't just one lizard-thing or gremlin, but a wave of creatures pouring down the staircase nearest the front door.

The girls pressed against the wall under their tent of velvet, crouched uncomfortably and shaking at the knees.

Grace held her breath as she watched green and blue feet scamper past, only inches from the edge of the velvet.

'There's none!' she heard a high-pitched voice cry in disappointment. 'Where are they all? There's none.'

'You scared them off,' another voice said with a titter. 'They saw your face.'

There was more giggling and scuffling as the owners of those blue and green feet appeared to tussle and then scurry away as something bigger approached. Grace couldn't see it at all, but its shadow covered the floor and its breathing wheezed and rattled like wind through a rusty wind chime.

'Hiding.' A voice to her right made her stomach squirm. It was like an old door, creaking with eerie musical notes. 'They've snuck away and are hiding in dark corners. But they cannot run.'

'My aboraceous friend is right.' This voice was slurpy, like water slopping in a trough. 'The witch-oags must be in hiding within the castle walls, but might I stress, dear friends, that it is not the young ones that hold the power here. The Three took the island. To take back the home, we must find the Three.'

'But the young ones are so tender and juicy.' The creaking voice snickered and loudly licked his lips.

The slurpy voice didn't laugh, but others did. Grace felt an

233

urgent need to pee. She crossed her legs beneath the curtain, twisting the fistful of Delilah's jumper in her hand. Beneath the material she could feel her friend's narrow shoulders trembling.

The creatures were spreading out through the corridors, whooping and squealing as they ran through the empty passageways. Several bodies scuffed past the curtain and it shifted in the girls' hands, but still they went unnoticed. Until…

'What do I see?' the creaking voice whispered. 'A little foot. One juicy little foot.'

Grace looked down in horror at her left shoe, out beyond the safety of the curtain. She snapped it back under the velvet but the damage was done.

'I know where the witch-oags are.' The voice was getting closer. 'I know where they've gone to hide. They think I can't see them there, but they don't know they're in plain sight!'

The curtain was whipped away and, before them, stood the owner of the creaking voice. He looked like the gremlin that attacked Adie, but much taller, with fleshy bulbs protruding between the black splinters of his arms, legs and neck. His yellow, needle-toothed grin stretched beyond the width of his cheeks, as if detached from his face and his long, pointed tongue slithered noisily over his lips.

'Let the feasting begin.'

'No!' Grace shrieked. She looked pleadingly at several

other faeries that remained in the reception hall. One, with a long face, elongated, bent limbs and a body like a mushroom stalk, frowned and regarded her carefully. 'We're not who you want. We haven't done anything wrong. *Please*!'

'Mmm, tasty morsels, I love it when they cry,' said the gremlin. 'They're keeping bad company and now they must *die*.'

He snatched her wrist, his grip like a vice. She squealed in pain and shock as his jaws stretched wide.

'Please, we just want to get home. We don't belong here. We're not who you're looking for!'

'I think you'll find,' a sing-song voice behind them made the gremlin stop suddenly, his mouth open, 'that this par-ticular group are considered outcasts amongst witch-kind. If it's revenge upon the Three you seek, these witch-oags will make a less than satisfying meal.'

The gremlin glared at the tall, shaggy beast that stood in the passageway.

'And who are you?'

The mushroom faery stepped between the two.

'Years, centuries,' he whispered earnestly. 'You are too young to remember, aboraceous, but this is the Phooka. And he has been missed.'

The Phooka smiled, an odd look on a goat, and held open his shaggy arms to the mushroom faery, who stretched up on his spindly limbs and hugged him warmly, dark streams staining his white, oval face.

'You have been missed,' the creature whispered again.

'Witches are witches,' the big gremlin snarled, ignoring the reunion, 'dinner is dinner, and meat is meat. The Three are not here, these creatures are, and I want to eat.'

'I met them in the dungeons.' The Phooka looked at the girls, and Grace still felt uneasy under the stare of those yellow eyes. 'They defied the Three and were punished. I freed them myself; a little indulgence to irk the Three before my strength is fully restored. But then I owed them something. They have a little pet that was of some assistance to me.'

The scattering of other faeries in the hall murmured curiously as the little wood nymph crawled from Delilah's collar, standing on her shoulder and swinging on her earlobe. He grinned at the other creatures, giving each of them a good view of his teeth that were finally losing their pink stain.

'Fascinating,' said the mushroom faery. He crept forward to tickle the wood nymph under the chin. 'He seems quite attached.' He glanced at the nymph's firm grip on Delilah's ear. 'Literally.'

The big gremlin bristled.

'A tiny-brained nymph, just a little brown rogue, will not come between me and delicious witch-oags.'

'You underestimate your dryad kin, my friend. Wood nymphs are suspicious by nature, and mischievous by heart. This is a bond not easily formed.' The mushroom faery looked deep into Delilah's big, brown eyes and smiled a little. 'If she has his friendship, then she has earned it.'

He sighed and stood up somewhat, keeping his knees bent.

'I think we can turn these little ones loose. They are no threat to us.'

The big gremlin scowled, but didn't stop the girls as they scooted to the front door, keeping their backs against the wall.

'Thank you,' Grace breathed.

She noticed Jenny giving the Phooka an uncertain wave, though he didn't respond.

Through the door and into the open air felt like impossible freedom. Grace squinted against the green hue that suffused the landscape, but was grateful to feel the sun on her skin.

They were crossing the dry, cracked rock, halfway to the woods, when they heard the dreadful scrape of wood on stone. Behind them the big gremlin had slunk from the castle, his black, fractured limbs scratching on the rock as he made his way – moving on four legs, then two, then four again – towards them. The pale lumps of flesh dotted over his body bobbed and shook as he moved.

Then something caught his eye. He froze, staring at something in the distance to his right and, just like that, he was scrambling back to the castle.

The girls didn't stop to see what had terrified him into retreat. They just ran for the safety of the woods and the promise of home.

no waiting

Tithon Castle was infested. It looked like some defenceless animal, swarmed by locusts that crawled up its face, into its eyes and ears. Rachel felt sick. Faeries filled the grounds and clung to the stone walls and, even some distance away, she could hear a wave of terrible sound; growling and screeching, the smacking of lips.

'Hurry,' she called to the Hunter at the helm. 'Please, hurry!'

She shuddered as she watched the barricaded windows on the ground floor being cleared by the creatures, and the hordes in the castle grounds disappearing inside the building. In her peripheral vision, she caught a glimpse of something blue.

It was a water sprite standing right beside her and smiling.

She was nonplussed for a moment until another one popped up in front, and then another. The Hunters were doing what Hunters did best. They would infiltrate the castle undercover of glamour, and attack the faeries from within.

The ship finally slowed, its keel grinding into the rock below. Rachel watched Aruj tuck the magical nuke into the leather baldric that crossed from his shoulder to his waist, before he glamoured himself into a tall, wiry beast. She took several deep breaths, but doubted she could hold any glamour of her own for more than a few minutes. She was still shaky from the trauma of the woods and the flame-running that caught the Hunters' attention. She needed rest, but there was no time.

Gripping the gunwale she readied herself to glide from the ship as soon as it was stationary, but several faeries running from the castle made her pause. There were five smaller faeries, and one large gremlin behind. Wait, they weren't faeries....

'Grace!' she screamed at the top of her lungs. 'Jennnny!'

They didn't hear her, but the gruesome thing that followed them stared in her direction, then hot-footed it back to the castle. The girls disappeared into the woods.

What time was it? Was she too late? Could she catch them?

Her tiredness forgotten, Rachel vaulted over the timber gunwale, slowing her fall just enough to ensure an untidy landing and no broken legs. She could hear Alinda calling for her in a worried voice, but she didn't look back. It was now or never.

With the sound of her own breath pounding in her ears, she wondered how she could ever have considered not going home. Now that it was just ahead of her – this one chance almost within her reach – she wanted it so badly it made her head swim. She wanted to see her family. She wanted her dad's chicken curry for dinner. She wanted to walk through the school gates and know that her friends would be there. She wanted to laugh with them, and annoy them, and complain about Mrs Quinlan's smelly kitchen with them.

She pulled open the leather jerkin that was too tight over her cotton blouse. It was just dressing-up. That's all the Hunters' Mansion had been, a game of make-believe. But the game was over now, and she was ready to go home.

The forest seemed lighter somehow. Even over the rushing feet of her friends, Grace could hear birdsong and scuffling in the bushes and trees. Empty of faeries, the place felt and sounded like the woods in Dunbridge.

Dunbridge.

Home.

The sun was climbing in the sky, dappling the girls with sunlight, and the higher it got, the more the chance of ever going home slipped through their fingers. They had to hope

Rachel was already there, and that she would stall the Ferry-man if they were late.

The little wood nymph nestled into the curve at the back of Delilah's neck, grinning at Grace. She growled at him, but found that her irritation spurred her on, and that she was keeping perfect pace behind the small girl. Jenny was further on, her powerful legs speeding ahead of the others. Grace didn't call her back. The sooner one of them got to the pebble beach, the better.

She could hear Una's laboured breaths as she pounded beside her and could feel her pain. P.E. was a dreaded subject for both of them, and they avoided this kind of gut-wrenching exercise like the plague.

'I can see!' Jenny's voice was strangled with exertion. 'I can see it ... it's up ahead. Come on!'

She disappeared into a final coppice of trees and the others raced after her.

Grace's ankle squirmed painfully to one side as the solid forest floor softened into sandy clay and then turned to pebbles. But she ran on, making for the mist-shrouded figure on the ferry. They were just metres away when Jenny stopped dead.

'She's not here,' she exclaimed, turning back to the others. 'Rachel's not here.'

The perpetual mist thickened over the water, but was thin enough on land for Grace to see for some distance. There was no-one else on shore.

'She's late,' she said, almost to herself. 'But she'll be here.'

But she didn't believe it. The sun was rising in the sky – and Rachel should have made it in good time. Something was very wrong.

She felt the sharp edges of the gemstone flower beneath her jumper, and wondered if they could bargain for time.

'No bargain,' the rusty voice of the Ferryman drifted through the fog, as if he had read her mind. 'No waiting.'

The waves licked at her feet. She felt like a bag of sand with a hole in one corner; energy drained out of her and her eyelids grew heavy.

'Delilah,' she said cautiously. 'Can you …? Are you feeling tired?'

'It's the water,' the girl replied, rubbing her eyes. 'It's like it's sucking all the life-force out of us. I won't be able to do any …' she lowered her voice and glanced to the Ferryman, '*tricks* to keep him here.'

'Departure,' the raspy voice sounded again. 'Have you the payment?'

'We need a minute,' Grace said urgently.

'Departure,' he repeated. 'Have you the payment?'

'We have it.' Grace whipped the sapphire rose out from under her jumper. 'But we have one more passenger. We need to wait.'

'No waiting.'

242

The Ferryman's sinewy hands pulled the end of the lamp-pole out of the sea-bed with a *ssslurp*, over his hooded head and back into the water. He started to push the boat from the shore.

'Nooo!'

Grace lunged and grabbed hold of the bow, stepping shin-deep into the water.

'Oh,' she swooned as the cool liquid grasped at her ankles, sapping what was left of her energy.

She instantly felt like she had been without sleep for days, weeks. She fell forward over the hull, dropping the blue rose into the bottom of the boat.

'Here,' she gasped, 'we have payment. But please …'

'Grace!'

Adie's voice came from behind as the rest of her slipped over the damp timber and onto the ferry. She felt Jenny's heavy step land beside her, and squeals and yells as the other three were pulled aboard.

Out of the water, Grace's head began to clear. Her friends were around her, wheezing and struggling against the energy-sapping effects of the seawater. Jenny was the only one standing. She held one of the Ferryman's shrouded arms, gritting her teeth with effort, while he continued to punt the boat out to sea. Grace clambered to her feet and grabbed his other arm, but his limbs were like the arms of some great machine; solid and unstoppable. He worked away, oblivious to their efforts.

✳ ✳ ✳

'She's there, I see her!' Adie pushed past Jenny, pointing wildly and almost toppling over the bow. 'There's Rachel! Can't you see her? On the beach?'

Through the mist Grace saw a figure in boots and a leather jerkin. She recognised the sleek, dark hair immediately.

'She's here!' she screamed at the Ferryman's hood. 'She's made it. Go back!'

But the arms didn't stop moving.

'Stop!' Jenny joined in, still pulling against the machine-like arms. 'She's here, you have to go back!'

But the boat didn't stop. Rachel stood on shore, waving and shouting. Grace's fists clenched and unclenched as she stood on the bow, helpless.

Out of the corner of her eye, she saw Delilah grab something from the stern and wrap it around herself.

'Throw me,' the small girl said, tying the rope swiftly around her waist.

'*What*?'

'THROW ME.'

Without another second's hesitation, Jenny and Grace grabbed an arm and leg each, ran the few steps they had room for, and launched the tiny girl into the air. The other end of the rope was tied to a cleat on the stern and, as the coils of braided hemp ran out, Grace saw the sharp pull on

Delilah's waist as she landed in the water. Rachel waded in up to her waist, and reached for the small girl paddling ahead of her.

Grace held her breath as Rachel's and Delilah's hands reached further and further, getting closer and closer. Their fingers touched. They were going to make it. They were all going to make it home. They were *all* safe …

No!

A sudden movement of the boat on a wave and Delilah was jerked out of Rachel's grasp.

No!

Rachel strove to get closer to the small girl, but she was getting out of her depth.

No deeper, Grace thought, though she wanted to scream the opposite. *No deeper – not in this water. It'll drown you.*

As if she had heard, Rachel suddenly turned and swam back, her head dipping underwater more than once.

As if on automatic pilot, Grace and Jenny pulled Delilah back to the boat, lifting her, gasping and spluttering, to the safety of the deck.

Far away, their friend crawled from the waves to the shore, collapsing onto one hip and looking back over her shoulder. Through the fog, Grace could still see Rachel's face. That lovely face. One by one, she felt hands clutch her jumper. Jenny, Adie, Delilah and Una gripped hands, tighter and tighter, so tight Grace lost feeling in her fingers. They clung to each other and watched their friend, alone on the beach, until the mist swallowed her up and there was nothing.

The fog was swimming, swirling, spreading apart into clumps of dark grey. Behind it was starry black. Grace groaned and turned her face to the heavens. Shiny, iron claws reached for the sky. Her head spun and the claws became the ugly wrought-iron twists on top of the gates of Dunbridge Cemetery. It was night-time. The sky was cloudy but there was no rain.

She was lying on the ground between two rows of grave-stones and she wasn't sure how she got there. She heard the *sshh* of gentle waves and leaned up on her elbows to look past her feet. The fog was thick, moving away as if blown by a giant bellows. The water – the sea – beneath it swept back across the graveyard, disappearing into the night. And in the mist a hooded figure piloted a boat by lamplight.

The Ferryman.

We're home, Grace thought, her mind clearing. *This is Dunbridge.*

Her friends were scattered around her, all struggling to their feet as they figured out where they were. Grace saw Adie's face light up in recognition of home, then suddenly crumple as the realisation hit them both at the same time. None of them broke the silence of the cemetery; they just stood and let the grief fall between them. Grace held the moment for as long as she could, because once she moved, it would be moving on without *her*. The second they left this spot, Rachel would be behind them. They would go to Mrs Quinlan and Ms Lemon; they would search all the ancient books in Mr Pamuk's shop, and Grace would scour every webpage on the internet that made any mention of *Hy-Breasal* or a faery island. They would search for a way to bring her home if it took the rest of their lives.

But Grace remembered the pure astonishment on Mrs Quinlan's and Ms Lemon's faces when that weird tube began sucking the girls from their own world. They hadn't known what it was or where it was taking them.

The graveyard was cold, but Grace held her arms out from her sides so she would feel it more. She heard the flutter of a bird's wings, even though it was so late, and a crow landed on a stone cross a few feet away. It eyed the girls curiously, then took off with a loud squawk. The moment was over.

Grace moved first, walking forward with her hands held out. Jenny took one, Adie took the other. Delilah and Una joined the line on either side and all five girls walked through the gates. The little wood nymph scurried up and down their arms, and across their shoulders, but Grace barely felt him. Turning onto the black tarmac of the road she paused. The avenue stretched ahead of them,

247

moonlit and long. Still without a word they moved forward together, and Grace felt a tear in her heart for every step they took.

beneath the glamour

Rachel cleared the forest before she knew she was running. She had sat there, on the pebble beach, the wicked water soaking into her clothes and sapping the energy from her limbs. She wasn't sure how long she had stayed there, watching the horizon, hoping the ferry would turn back and collect her from the shore. The sensation of Delilah's fingertips on hers plagued her and made her nose sting with tears. They were so close; an inch, one single inch more, and Rachel would be on that boat sailing for home.

She didn't remember getting to her feet, or stumbling across the rounded pebbles to the woods. She didn't remember the new sounds of the forest or the sunlight that streamed through the trees. She didn't remember making the decision to return to the castle but, when she finally emerged on the cracked, parched rock, she knew where she was, and why she was there.

She closed her eyes and raised her face to the sun, as if the rays could revitalise her tired body. When she opened them again, it was the first time she didn't feel the need to squint against that green tint that drenched everything in this world. Wide-eyed and feeling stronger than she had in ages, she picked up her feet and jogged swiftly towards the castle grounds.

There was eerie quiet when she pushed open the studded oak door into the reception hall, and a quick glance at the floor told her why. She grimaced, turning away from the faery bodies that lay scattered across the stone. Blue skin, wiry hair, clawed hands; she couldn't help snatching glances as she stepped gingerly between them. She wriggled her fingers, trying to erase the memory of sticky sap spilling over her hand and the dying hiss of the gremlin in the Hunters' Mansion. It seemed childish now, that she had ever thought that life desirable.

The corridor wasn't completely clear, but there were thankfully fewer bodies the further she went, though the occasional sight of a privateer's shirt or sword sent a shiver up her spine. The Hunters had made it quite far into the castle before the faeries noticed the intrusion and began taking out those creatures that were attacking their own. The witches that lay slain in the passageway, she knew, were those that dropped their glamour first. It wasn't until she reached the entrance to the arena that she finally heard any sound – the sound of discontented muttering.

Creeping around the door jamb, she froze to the spot. The faeries were spread out across the bleachers and the playing field, staring and tense and wary. The atmosphere crackled with hostility. The Supremes stood frazzled and nervous on one side, guarded by gremlins, with several Hunters nearby, bound and kneeling. Rachel gasped when she noticed Alinda among them.

So few witches were caught, Rachel realized, because the Hunters were still hidden in the crowd. Faeries snarled and snapped at each other, and the air was thick with suspicion. If this went on for much longer, she was sure the faery army would tear itself apart. And maybe that was what the Hunters wanted.

The Fungi stood on the lower platform, his long bony hand extended and appealing for calm. He scrutinised the faces of those around him and, given time, Rachel thought he could probably discern the real faeries from the fakes. But time was not on his side. The arena smouldered like oil left on a hot pan, spitting and smoking, and ready to catch fire at any moment. Beside the Fungi, a goat-like beast lounged luxuriously on the wooden boards. He seemed unaffected by the drama. In fact, he seemed to be soaking it all in with amused interest. Rachel wondered what he had to be so happy about.

251

One of the ugly gremlins snapped at Alinda, making her jump. The gremlin laughed cruelly, but the woman simply shook her silver hair, the plaits loosening around her face, and stared at him defiantly. The situation was not going to resolve itself; not in any way that Rachel could bear to watch. So she swallowed hard and stepped forward – not glamouring, not protecting herself in any way – and walked into the arena towards the ancient faery on the platform.

Drops of spittle sprayed her cheek as the creatures hissed and slurped and growled at her. A guarding gremlin had lurched forward to pin her, but was stayed by a wave from the Fungi. His reaction made the crowd part in curiosity, allowing her to approach the platform. But all those tense muscles, full of spite and aggression, made her feel totally unsafe. She stood before the Fungi and his shaggy goat companion and spoke.

'This can only end badly, for everyone.' She gestured around the arena and ignored the wheezy laughter from the gruffer beasts. 'I know that's not what you all want.'

The Fungi watched her carefully.

'What would you propose?'

'A truce.'

More wheezy laughter.

'And what about justice?'

252

'You have the Three, don't you?' Rachel said, glancing to the Supremes still under guard. She felt guilty saying it, but she felt she had no choice. 'Do what you want with them, and let the rest go.'

The Supremes were a sorry-looking spectacle. Lord Machlau's tweed lapels drooped sadly towards the ground, his stooped frame rigid and uncomfortable-looking as always. Even if he felt the desire to look someone in the eye, he was incapable of doing it. Lady Hecate's tightly bound hair was coming undone, and a few grey hairs were now visible. Despite her once-imposing height, she stood like a frightened child, head bowed and hands shaking. Whatever great power she had was long gone.

And Madame Three. Her clenched fists held handfuls of ash; she looked at them intermittently like she didn't know what she was holding, then as if she suddenly remembered, would clasp them mournfully to her chest.

Rachel suspected the woman had already abandoned the elixir that kept her body going well beyond its lifetime. Her unnaturally plump face now sagged with the weight of so many years, her stout form was shrinking under the swathes of velvet cloak, and her blonde hair was thinner than Rachel remembered, losing its tight curls and falling in skinny waves down her neck.

Rachel watched the Fungi's expression and understood his disappointment. What revenge could he wreak on the

Supremes that would be worse than what they had done to themselves?

'And what of the others?' he asked. 'Those that stand amongst my kin with masks and disguises, waiting and watching. Ready to kill and maim.'

Rachel turned to the crowd.

'Look around you,' she called. 'Look how many there are. I saw the faery bodies in the castle, but I saw the Hunters too. If you let this go on, it'll just be carnage. You'll all die here today, and for what? You won't protect the witch-oags that need your help, you won't live on to share the Hunters' legacy with anyone, you'll just end.' She clasped her hands. 'Why not a truce? Why would peace be so bad? There's plenty of room on this island, isn't there? *Isn't there?*'

No-one responded, but there was silence. They were listening.

Rachel felt hope until she turned to Alinda and saw a small, ghostly boy kneeling next to the woman, curling a strand of her silver hair in his fingers.

'Revenge,' Alinda whispered.

'There's nothing to take revenge for,' Rachel said gently. 'He's not a real child.'

Tormey Vause smiled at her, still twisting the lock of hair.

'I see you.' Rachel stared into his wicked face. 'I see what you really are.'

She was telling the truth. The more she stared, the more

the dark circles under his eyes and around his mouth spread across his white skin. His big, soft eyes disappeared, his small childish limbs lengthened into shadowy claws. He was like a black hole. So dark and so deep that you could fall in and get lost.

'You may see,' the Fungi said. 'But weaker minds are easily led.'

Rachel turned back to the crowd with tears in her eyes.

'You're good people, Hunters. You're kind and brave, and you deserve more than this.'

She shuddered as more of the Lost Ones appeared in the congregation, taking the hands of glamoured Hunters; the fake faeries looked down at the children with glassy eyes. A few seconds more of this and there would be all out war.

'Kill them.'

The voices were quiet and gentle and pushing.

'Kill them.'

'No!' Rachel shouted. 'Look at them. *Look* at them. Look deep into their eyes and see them for what they really are. There are NO Lost Ones, there is NO Tormey Vause. You're stronger than this, Hunters, I know you are. *Please!*'

There was no sound, no agreement.

'Please,' Rachel said again, her voice cracking. 'Please, trust me.'

More silence.

'A shadow.'

It was barely a whisper, to her left. Rachel spun and watched Alinda's pale eyes grow wide.

'I see a shadow.' The woman slowly got to her feet, making the gremlins behind her snarl and snap, but she didn't heed them. She stared deep into the spirit of Tormey Vause and her breath quickened.

'I see it. *I see* it!'

Tormy Vause's form warped back into Rachel's view, but his milk teeth were now pointed and long. He hissed angrily. To her right she saw a faery jump, and drop the hand of Lark Walden, and his own glamour. The Hunter beneath looked shocked and afraid. There was more scuffling in the crowd as Hunters backed away from the dark spirits beside them that now hissed and spat in anger.

She scanned the crowd for one faery in particular. If she didn't find him, this could all be for nothing.

Behind her she could hear Alinda's cries for a truce, and the Fungi's call for calm.

Still she couldn't find the creature she needed.

Until she spotted him. Deep in the crowd, still holding fast to the hand of Vela Romwood, stood Aruj, cloaked in glamour. Vela watched him, her expression encouraging, as he smiled down at her. Then the tall, wiry beast dropped her hand and sprinted for the platform.

His strong arms pushed through the mass, sending creatures flying left and right. He was nearly upon them. Rachel had a couple of seconds and no longer. She kept her gaze fixed on his narrow, red eyes, the buzz playing up and down her fingers. She had to time this right. She had to catch him off guard.

He made one last push, leaping forward, and she leapt with him. The glamour swallowed Rachel's appearance and she met him mid-air as the Fungi. A fleeting look of surprise, then he grinned and grabbed her shoulders. They hit the ground rolling as he reached for his chest, but she was quicker than him. She couldn't see it, but she knew the nuke was there, lodged in the leather baldric strapped to his torso.

She felt it, oval and hot, and snatched it from the strap. He howled in surprise as she spun out of his grip, his glamour fading and three gremlin guards landing on him from behind. Rachel rolled to safety and hugged the orange-red jewel to her tummy. She stayed kneeling by the platform until the ruckus died down, one side urged by Alinda and the other by the real Fungi to keep from attacking.

Rachel closed her eyes against the noise and felt the shuddering power of the spessartine gem, wrapped in twists of orgonite, as her glamour faded. When she finally opened them, the quiet was uneasy, but it was there.

'And the witch-oags?' Alinda said to the Fungi, as if mid-conversation. 'Have you—?'

'In the dungeons, I think you'll find.' The big goat thing hadn't moved from his spot on the platform. He still lounged comfortably, leaning back on his elbows and grinning. 'Clever little minxes hid underground.'

Alinda heaved a sigh of relief.

'Then–'

'Then of course they will remain safe,' the Fungi interrupted. 'As will my kin that remain standing here. Yes?'

'Yes.'

'Then let our peoples return to their homes, while you and I discuss the best and most mutual agreement.'

'I think that sounds fair.'

Alinda traced her fingers down Aruj's cheek as he was transferred from the custody of gremlins, to Hunter guards.

'I'll free you yet, cousin.'

He snarled at her betrayal, but Rachel was sure the silver-haired woman could make him see the shadows eventually. Even if she couldn't, the dark spirits had already lost some of their power and would lose more in time. With a truce in place, there would be balance amongst the spirits of the island. Rachel smiled as she tried to imagine what the light spirits looked like.

'I dread to ask what that object is,' said an ancient, tired voice.

The Fungi stood over Rachel on his spindly, bent legs.

'This?' Rachel held fast to it and smiled. 'This is mine.'

'Very well, I'll ask no more.' He held out one long bony hand. 'My thanks to you, little asrai.'

She shook it and nodded to Alinda behind him, who smiled sadly. Then, holding the magical nuke to her lips, Rachel whispered her greatest wish. The world shook and shattered, but she wasn't afraid.

✦ ✦ ✦

Grace stood outside the window of Mrs Quinlan's front room. It was packed with junk and as messy as she remembered. Weird, stuffed animals leered with fixed, glassy eyes, an old piano sat smothered in dust and cobwebs, and there were trunks and boxes everywhere. Their contents had been tipped onto the floor in haste – ancient books and pages and scrolls – lying scattered amongst torn and crumpled bits of paper. Mrs Quinlan had been searching, searching for a way to bring them home.

She was slumped over an old-fashioned school desk in one corner, fast asleep. She held a quill pen in one hand and her fingers were stained with ink. She looked older than before, her grey hair falling in matted clumps over her face, and she was snoring so loudly Grace could hear her from outside the house.

'I wonder how long she's been cooped up in there,' Jenny whispered.

'Days,' Grace replied. 'Look at that mess.'

They watched through the glass and felt guilty. Even in her sleep the woman looked worried. How could they wake her now and reveal they had returned home – but that one of them was missing? They stood in the dark and listened to the hypnotic drone of Mrs Quinlan's snores.

'So are you going in, or what?'

Grace's heart nearly stopped. That voice, she knew that voice! She turned to the end of the driveway.

'Rachel!'

She looked like something out of a fairytale. Her leather jerkin was open over her cotton blouse, and the moonlight played on her shiny, dark hair that was falling out of its plait. She held something in her hands, but after a quick glance at it, tossed it into the parched grass of Mrs Quinlan's lawn.

'Rachel! Oh, Rachel!'

Adie ran first, her black curls flying behind her as she wrapped her arms around the girl's neck. Delilah and Una followed, and when Jenny finally ploughed into the mass hug they all toppled to the ground. Grace walked slowly down the driveway and stood over them, watching with tears in her eyes as her friends giggled and squealed, and moaned when one of them got an elbow in the stomach.

This was it. This was real. They were all, finally, *home*.

She tipped forward onto the pile of bodies, ignoring Una's yelling as she was squished under her weight, and cried her eyes out.

'Who's out there?' a voice yelled from the door. 'Who is that?'

The girls scrambled to their feet, still giggling and sighing, and smiled at the Old Cat Lady filling the doorway.

'We're home, Mrs Quinlan,' Una said loudly. 'We made it.'

The woman just stood with her mouth wide open. Finally, she stumbled forward and grabbed hold of Delilah, crushing the girl against her moth-eaten robe, and jumping as the little wood nymph clambered out and grinned at her. Delilah wriggled out of Mrs Quinlan's vice-like grip and grasped the nymph around the waist, sitting him on her shoulder. She smiled up at her guardian, pulling a stray cat hair out of her mouth.

Mrs Quinlan stared down at them, still in shock, then pointed into the house.

'Phone,' she said quickly. 'I have a phone.'

She snapped when no-one replied.

'To phone your parents. I have a phone!'

In the whole time that they'd known her, Mrs Quinlan had scoffed at any form of technology, and never had a phone in the house.

'Actually,' Jenny said, pulling her mobile from her pocket, 'I think we've got signal now, so we can just–'

'I got a phone!' the woman yelled again. 'For this. I got a phone for this! It's in the hall. Now, go and ring your parents.'

'Okay then.' Jenny smiled at Grace. 'I'll go first.'

'Do you know how to use it?' the woman barked, following her into the house, and keeping a grip around

Delilah's shoulders.

'Yeah, yeah, I know how to use it.'

'You wait for a dial tone …' Mrs Quinlan's voice disappeared into the hallway.

Una and Adie burst out laughing.

'I know it's not funny. I know everyone's going to be crying, and it'll be horrible and brilliant at the same time,' Adie said, wiping a tear from her eye. 'But still. *A phone.*'

Una leaned on Adie's arm, still in stitches as they made their way into the house, leaving Grace and Rachel on the driveway.

Rachel went to pull her jerkin closed, then let it go.

'What's the point?' she said lightly, tugging at the falling mess that was her hair.

'I think you've never looked better,' said Grace.

They grinned at each other for a moment.

'Will you miss it?' Grace asked finally.

'You know,' Rachel said, linking her arm and walking her towards the house. 'I really won't.'

Neither will I, thought Grace.

She squinted against the light of the hall and listened to the always-arguing voices of Jenny and Mrs Quinlan and sighed. It was so good to be home.

Q and a

with
Erika McGann

Where did you get the idea for the first book in the series, *The Demon Notebook?*

From the memory of when my friends and I actually tried to do a pee spell on someone in school! The first book came from that one little incident. My friends and I were aspiring witches – but we were not good at it. Like Grace and her friends, we tried casting spells (that didn't work) and making potions (mostly smelly goo that also didn't work). I don't remember what all of the spells were, but I remember the pee spell. We tried to make a boy pee his pants in French class because he'd been mean to one of us. It didn't work, and we were absolutely gutted. But, looking back, I'm glad we were rubbish witches. I dread to think what would have happened if we'd gotten exactly what we wanted!

Who was your favourite author as a kid?

Roald Dahl. I still love his books. As a kid I adored reading them. They were so gross and impolite and grotesque, it felt like I was reading something I shouldn't, yet they were books that were bought for me by adults. And the kids in his stories always did cool stuff – they were outwitting witches, getting abducted by giants or moving things around with their minds – they were the ones with the cunning and the power. I loved that.

Do you ever get to meet your readers?

I do. I visit a lot of school groups in libraries during book festivals and other events, and I love it. Before I started, I thought talking to a big group of kids would be terrifying – I thought they'd heckle me and make me cry – but I haven't run crying from a library yet. Kids are actually a brilliant audience. I love talking to them about reading, because I can talk about books like *I'm* a kid again. I don't have to be serious and sensible, I can be as enthusiastic as I want and get all hyper when someone loves the same books I do.

How long have you been writing?

I know I'm three books in now, but I still feel like a newbie. I haven't been slogging away at the craft for years like I'm supposed to have done. I wanted to be an author when I was very young, but I grew out of it as a teenager and didn't start writing again until my late twenties. So I've really only been doing it a few years. I hope I'm getting better as I go along.

What's the hardest thing about writing?

Being disciplined. That's really hard. Usually I sit down at my laptop, stare at the screen for a bit, then get up and make a cup of tea – I make a lot of tea when I'm writing – I also do the laundry, wash the dishes, surf the net, watch YouTube videos of animals who sound like they're speaking English … I can procrastinate with the best of them.

But when you do get into the swing of it – after the tea, and the laundry, and the springer spaniel saying 'I love you' – there's nothing like it. Getting some good writing done always feels great.

What advice would you give to budding writers?

First, write. Write and read – every day if you can. They go hand in hand and, the more you read, the more you'll write. It's also a good idea to keep a scrappy journal to jot down interesting ideas, snippets of overheard conversations, items from magazines or newspapers. It could all be raw material for a story.

Second, write what you enjoy. It can be very hard to get published, and there's always pressure to write what's most likely to sell. But if you're scribbling about something that doesn't really interest you, it's bound to show. And I always think, if you're not getting a kick out of what you're writing, then why do it at all?

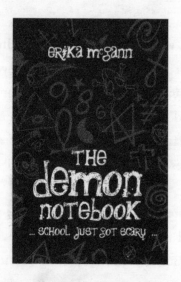

The Demon Notebook

Grace and her four best friends, Jenny, Rachel,
Adie and Una, are failed witches. But one night,
they stumble upon real magical powers – and their
notebook takes on a diabolical life of its own.

Can Grace and her friends stem the wave of powerful
magic … before tragedy strikes?

**Winner of the Waverton Good Read
Children's Award 2014**

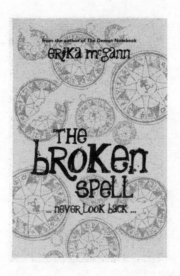

from the author of *The Demon Notebook*

ERIKA McGANN

THE
bROKEN
spell
... neveR LooK back ...

The Broken Spell

Trainee witch Grace and her four best friends love
to have fun with spells. But the daring friends make
a magical mistake that drags the past into the present.
Suddenly Grace has to work out who
she can really trust ...